The Prophet of Sorrow

�ખ ✕ ✕

To my cousin Don Williams & Family

Please enjoy my little book—

The Prophet of Sorrow

Mark Van Aken Williams

Mark V Williams

LUCKY PRESS, LLC
ATHENS, OHIO

Lucky Press, LLC. Est. 2000   www.LuckyPress.com
ISBN-13:978-0-9844627-0-4   ISBN-10: 0-9844627-0-8
Library of Congress Control Number: 2010902802

For trade purchase orders, contact:
614.413.2820 (fax)   sales@luckypress.com (email)   SAN: 850-9697

Author's website: www.markvawilliams.com
Book design: Janice Phelps, LLC

Cover image: David Alfaro Siqueiros, "The Sob," 1939 ©2010 Artist Rights
Society (ARS), New York/SOMAAP, Mexico City.
Digital Image © The Museum of Modern Art/Licensed by SCALA / Art Resource,
NY ART169271. Used with permission.

This book is a work of fiction. Names, characters, locations, and events either
are the product of the author's imagination or are used fictitiously, and any
resemblance to actual persons (alive or deceased), places, or events is entirely
coincidental.

Williams, Mark Van Aken.

   The prophet of sorrow / Mark Van Aken Williams. -- Athens, Ohio : Lucky
   Press, c2010.

      p. ; cm.

      ISBN: 13-digit: 978-0-9844627-0-4 ; 10-digit: 0-9844627-0-8

      1. Mercader del Río Hernández, Jaime Ramón, 1914- --Fiction. 2.
   Trotsky, Leon, 1879-1940--Assassination--Fiction. 3. Mexico--History--
   1910-1946--Fiction. 4. Assassins--Biography--Fiction. 5. Biographical fiction.
   6. Historical fiction. I. Title.

PS3623.I55866 P76 2010   2010902802

813.6--dc22   1005

To my wife, Janice

*"How meaningful it is that the glory
of mankind, upon him be peace and blessings,
who spent his life in sorrow, is rightly
described as the Prophet of Sorrow."*

~Necib Fazil

1

*T*wenty years ago I killed Leon Trotsky. I have spent the time since in the Lucumberri Prison in Mexico and now am the guest of Fidel Castro's government, here in Havana. I have lived many lives and have been known to others as Ramón Mercader, Jacques Mornard, Harold Jacson, Vandendreschd, and even Gnome. There are others that do not pertain to this story, and I'm sure that I will rest under a headstone with a name unfamiliar to me as yet.

The truculent deal is this: we are permitted a mercurial mind only when we don't know how to keep it in reserve; and we only learn how to bring it to terms when these gifts have departed. Along this line, we discover that we are not responsible for our own fate and destiny, but we are responsible for how we react to it. Our values are determined by the attitude we develop toward our destined and irrevocable suffering. Our unresolved sorrows flow along a hidden expanse.

At one end have been the deaths that have caused the scarring and hardening, the peeling off of the masks of different legends, only to reveal a numb surface. The more I let go of my identities, the more I die to myself in uncircumscribed humility, and the less I have to defend.

*A*t the other end, I am a boy in Barcelona living with my mother, Eustacia María Caridad del Río Hernandez, after she separated from my father. Life for workers and peasants in Spain in the 1920s and 1930s was bad, and if you were a woman it was even worse. Mother's wedding was pre-arranged and she had no independence.

She took me to France and I was raised there. Mother was smart and attractive. Her intelligence brought her, and consequently me, into contact with many intellectuals. Change begins with discussion and, through the messy process of debate and disagreement, our world view can be radically altered.

Back in Spain, the socialist UGT union federations were taking to the streets. They aimed to empower women and believed that it was crucial to involve them directly in the struggle for liberation. Revolution was starting in Spain as a reaction to the military coup. Spanish women did not see themselves as enfranchised and most of them had in fact never even heard of it, yet their response was spontaneous and courageous.

My mother had become a confirmed socialist and an activist, but her strong personality drew her towards Stalinism for one reason and one reason only: Leonid Eitingon.

She was faced with the sense of necessity to choose between fascism and anti-fascism back in Spain — the same force that was propelling so many other Spaniards into the arms of the Communist Party.

Eitingon was introduced to mother, who was called Caridad by her friends, as the head of business operations for the Soviet Fur Trust and was extremely handsome, with grey-green eyes and a full head of black hair. He seduced her with his polished weapons of humor and impertinence. But in fact, he was the NKVD's *(Narodnyi Komissariat Vnutrennikh Del)* outstanding expert in operations against Russian anti-Communist exiles, as well as Trotskyites.

Among Eitingon's special tasks was responsibility for sabotage, kidnapping, and assassination of the Soviet's enemies beyond the country's borders — helping Comrade Stalin protect and provide dignity for all workers and eliminate the rapacity and despotism of capitalist profit.

We packed our bags and headed from France back to Barcelona, where Eitingon assumed the role of a military attaché (General Katov) in the Soviet Consulate. Here he organized the persecution against the POUM (Workers Party of Marxist Unification), who were closely associated with Trotsky.

It was his role in the GPU (Communist Secret police or Cheka) that would change my life. This was Stalin's secret army. My mother and I were eventually trained as part of this group; training that set my destiny.

2

Leonid Eitingon: Notes (NKVD files) on Recruitment

*P*redictability *is the greatest source of unhappiness. Our expectations may be impractical. We may be able to influence but not control people and situations, or the future.*

When I was growing up my mother had the tendency to feed me with excruciating guilt for making any personal choices. Every gesture of affection or kindness returned, seemed to be executed with some degree of effort or burden. Any interest in girls was incessantly disapproved of, and she constantly interfered with my relationships. She would manipulate circumstances and situations to her own benefit and consideration, over my own happiness, independence, and individuation.

I have long held that this was most likely due to having no love from her own father and ultimately to receiving the same manner of Spanish paternal despotism from her husband my father; people incapable of reciprocating their feelings of love and devotion. This left her hollow and I was the one who compensated for that tragic loss. She had no choice but to latch on to me. I was her perfect child, partner, father, and lover. I learned at a very early age how to assume multiple identities. In a way, I also clung to her as my own eternal savior and undying icon of perfect love and immutable security.

Upon our return to Spain, women were involved everywhere in the initial resistance and fought equally among members of the anti-fascist militias up until November 1936, when they were ordered away from the frontlines. Many had been killed in the battled for Madrid. As the war went on, they became increasingly involved with the housing, care, and education of the refugees. The socialists, Communists, and POUM all set up women's sections. Each side was trying to draw women into the struggle via their own organizations. I mention all this because the fate of women, not unlike my mother, was closely tied to that of the overall Revolution.

As the Revolution was pushed back by the Communist Party and the government, so was the fate of women in Spain.

Before Eitingon seduced and recruited Caridad, this fate, which was spanning her long-unattended sorrows, was gradually closing her down: the slowly accumulating burdens of defeated expectations and blighted hope, the loss of certainty, conviction, and confidence that decreases along the spectrum — until at the far end we start to sink in the bog of lost hope and are barely able to reach out for extrication. She was unable to find herself until Eitingon empowered her to reenter those parts of herself long since abandoned to hopelessness and vulnerability.

Caridad Mercader: Barcelona 1936

When we lose or never use what we need or love, we call this diminuendo of our intellectual curiosity "suffering." It comes with the loss of dignity due to a multitude of finely effectuated cultural humilities. This has given rise to my most notable griefs and has caused me a considerable amount of anger and initiative. In order to overcome my feelings of having no control, I have decided to assert whatever power I can to hide the fear and sense of profound insularity.

I used to believe that happiness and unhappiness could be separated, implying that good and evil were separate entities and would always remain so. I now know that this is an illusion. Good and evil are enleagued. The Christian conceptions of the Church in Spain, of what is pious and deferential, have always had their origins in that which is evil.

If I make happiness the aspiration of my life, it will only elude me. It is something that only steals through the back door when we devote ourselves to the cause of something that is significant.

I believe that becoming an agent of the GPU will be costly and risky, but I have no doubt that in this endeavor I will discover what makes life worth living, even in the face of suffering and death.

Leonid wants me to recruit Ramón. I know he will follow me. He has always been a good boy. He joined the Communist Party in 1933 when it was already a Stalinist party.

3

In Barcelona, I had joined the Communist Party. I was only carrying out small tasks and my talents were not being effectively used. In spite of this, I was slowly working my way up the Party hierarchy. This seemed easy for me because of my ability to manipulate circumstances or people to make ends meet and to achieve contentment. I learned long ago how to do this, by sidestepping my mother's covert and overt disapprovals and her constant blaming of friends and lovers as being inadequate or weak. Of course I would never voice objections to her about this, yet I believed that my strong personality came from compensating for the profound sense of insolidity I felt when younger. Not only was my personality suited for what I was doing, but it was eclipsing everyone else in my ranks, up to that point.

I found it important to devote all of my energies to my work, because it was difficult to fit in with groups of peers or establish lasting relationships. When I did find someone that I thought I would like, inevitably I found it difficult to commit to her in an intimate way. Who wouldn't understand? My fidelity was toward my mother who was starting to become a very important person in Stalin's private army. Eitingon and Mother were spending much more time with me. I couldn't help but be impressed with her. In silence I suffered from incestuous feelings, which were in dark contrast to the intrusive way she was prioritizing my life. In the end, I decided that it was more important to sacrifice personal values and objectives in accordance to Mother's expectations and wishes.

Leonid Etingon: Notes (NKVD files) on Recruitment, Barcelona

amón Mercader looks like a likely candidate for our purposes. His personality type seems to be one of no particular individuation, yet he is intelligent. He has not been able, as an adult, to break the bondage of his mother's wishes, wants, issues, and complexes.

This relationship will be of value to us, in that we should be able to influence him through her. He has not figured out his own path. He has great devotion and diligence towards her. He is not yet a man because of this, nor is he yet an individual. Many of his unique attributes are still inscribed in his mother's womb. Perhaps the Soviet experiment can become a surrogate. And he can be reborn, where the unique aspects of our agenda will materialize.

He has a quest to give birth to himself, which is part of the progression — when evolving from boy to man. The guidance and outside help can come from us: a task that he will not be able to accomplish alone.

I perceive from him a grief that comes from unsatisfied desires and lost loves, and from the lacerating trajectory of impermanence in Spain and in the world. Things are within his reach and then pulled away.

We should be able to turn his perturbations outward and direct his negative feelings to others (of our choosing), who we will make clear to him are the cause of his discrepancies. It is easy to make others, like Ramón, change their identities and behaviors this way. When he turns inward, the self is the cause of discrepancies in life. The self needs to be motivated to manage these identities and behaviors. We will provide his motivation.

4

The rise of Fascism in Italy, global economic depression, and the Nazi revolution in Germany, were all having their effect in Spain. The Republican Army was formed in response to the overthrow of the elected government by General Francisco Franco, in July 1936. Many soldiers, who remained loyal to the government, were joined by various political groups, including the Communist-controlled Fifth Regiment. I had been imprisoned for my activities for a short time, but when I was released in 1936, I became an officer in the army. The Soviet Union was heavily involved, by now, through our local CP.

Some say that we make war in the back of our brains and make peace just behind the brow. Everything that was happening to me seemed to be predetermined by the attitude of the moment. My feelings of provocation seemed to follow as a result of a thwarting of my desires and attitudes, in a way that

I just couldn't quite articulate. It was there, but I couldn't touch it. It had an accumulative effect, where my previous failures became more intense in my memory than when they actually happened. I was becoming aware of a wounding type of anger that was building upon itself.

Eitingon was helpful. He started showing me how the Trotskyites in the POUM were the enemy of the Soviet Union and that Stalin was the only one who could ensure the future of the Party. Strangely enough, my newly acquired mental disposition toward Trotsky was bringing about a low self-feeling and consequently elicited a great deal of anger.

It is not what he wrote about or his views about the proletariat, that offended me, but it was his attitude about Stalin that bothered me so much. He was flaunting his intellectual superiority. I have always found too great a display of wisdom to be condescending.

I saw a man on the street one day who resembled Trotsky. At first I just stood there and watched him pass, and then I started to imagine myself knocking him down. He looked up at me with a look of astonishment and I started kicking him down the street. It was merely a mental reaction. Somehow, my inhibitions would never have allowed me to really do this, yet I felt as if my hostile tendencies had been successfully expressed. It felt good.

The image of this pugnacious attack stayed with me for awhile and I thought about it often. I finally concluded that it was the outcome of going through a period of feeling that there was nothing else to be done about my frustrations, at what seemed to be a moment of crisis in my life and in the country. This man became the substitute. I had complete control over him with what Wordsworth called, "that inward eye which is the bliss of solitude."

The more I thought about it, the more I began to see myself as his superior. The prospect of a bright future and successful career became clear. I could see myself in the course ahead, where I had gained renown, and it would be Trotsky who would be telling all that he knew me when I was just a small and insignificant member of the proletariat. A new level of self-confidence was coming to me, and this would have an important influence on me later.

It is said that anger can diminish or disappear with a change of attention. This happens when one's way of looking at things is changed by the addition of new ideas that will give an entirely new meaning to something. In many respects, anger can be cut off at its source.

Leonid Eitingon: Notes (NKVD files) on Recruitment

I have been spelling out for Ramón Mercader how his future should be in the services of the GPU. He is still young and immature, but with proper training we can turn him into a useful asset. I have begun to alleviate many of his anxieties by pointing out to him what exactly was going on inside of him. First: emotions are cognitive. We do not act blindly like animals. Our emotions are intelligent and discriminating parts of our personalities. They are closely related to beliefs, and are consequently responsive to modification. They can be changed. Secondly: emotions are evaluative. Not only are they judgments about the world, but also include one's judgments about how the world relates to us. And thirdly; emotions have intentionality. They are dependent on how one sees the object of his emotion. This involves complex beliefs about that object, which also means how that object fits into your life.

I have explained to him how we can identify these cognitive, evaluative and intentionality components in his personality, which will make him a valuable part of the Soviet experiment. Ramón wants to be just this: important.

I believe that he could be used for diversionary activities of the Soviet intelligence. I want to bring him, along with his mother, back to the Soviet Union to be trained and briefed in detail.

I have pointed out to both how their expectations are not being met, here in Spain; their expectations about the future, about themselves, and about others. Here, they only have allusions of control, and are unrealistically expecting the Revolution and all involved to turn out as they think it should. The anger over these unmet expectations will only lead them to blame the Party and shift their aggression towards it.

Leon Trotsky: Journal

Stalin cannot come to grips with the call for a Fourth International. He is scared of me. I truly believe this. The Revolution does not have the right to deprive the cause of my services. Of course I have had feelings of hopelessness and disillusionment, but I have endurance and tenacity. I will never abandon my intellectual convictions. And these are to lead the Communist Party away from bureaucratic degeneration and abandonment of Marxist–Leninism. We must return to our original traditions. The world is being infiltrated by the minions of Stalin to spread fear of the nascent dictator, all in the name of ambition and careerism.

What Stalin fears is the reaction of the masses in Russia to this call. What he doesn't understand is that if a few normal individuals can be led to rebel, the authorities should not necessarily worry about the number of people attempting to alter their situations. Even when the number of activists is large, relatively few members of underprivileged groups (those not a part of the bureaucracy) become involved in actions against those in power — the ones they see as responsible for their poor circumstances. This is why the fight has to be international. Stalin wants to contain it in Russia. That way he can control it.

Many believe that I am fighting a lost cause. But lost causes are the only ones worth fighting for. They are the most important and sympathetic ones. Of course it will require me to live up to the best that is in me. Even if it does not come about (I do not perfect myself and we do not perfect our world), I must nevertheless try, because it is such a crucial purpose.

This is not an absurdist comedy; in that play, one would recognize what a lost cause is and work on it anyway. I do not concede it as such.

One could say that the relationship between the Spanish republican government and the Stalinist bureaucracy originated out of the
fusion of equipollent interests. What is clear though, is that the civil
war in Spain will be lost if the Revolution is betrayed. I fear that this
will happen, because Stalin believes that the war in Spain is not a
socialist revolution but a defense of democracy. There are already
systematic kidnappings and murder by the Stalinist secret police of my
sympathizers in Barcelona taking place.

Joseph Stalin: Journal

Trotsky and his Left Opposition are trying to create discontent among the people, based on what people have in the Soviet Union and what they see as possible to have. I am convinced that the way to judge your effectiveness as a leader is to quantify the amount of discontent you engender. When expectations rise in a country, it becomes the source of the discontent and the engine for change. The potential for revolution and political violence depends on the scope and intensity of this discontent.

The problem for me is the gap between these expectations (that Trotsky is espousing) and the capability to satisfy the people. We need to keep these ideas from becoming widespread. We must snuff out their cumulative effects before it is too late.

It is widely accepted as self-evident that all men are created equal. But somewhere along the line, it does not work out when considering the desired actual equality of conditions.

Just as in nature, a disturbance of atmospheric equilibrium can cause catastrophic consequences. The storm can sweep through with a baneful power that is Cyclopean.

So this notion of equality is absolutely absurd — a dream. Discontentment arises not only from notions of equality, but also from the natural conditions of inequality. It is impossible to enlighten the people at this stage in our experiment, to their wish fulfillment, faster than social conditions can be accommodated, or perhaps can ever be sorted out to serve those wants.

Because of this, it is even more important to distract attention away from the nation's actual hardship and suffering.

We live in uncertain times. The world is unstable and imperma-nent. As the rest of the world struggles to find lasting pleasure, deeper *meaning, certainty and perfection, we realize here in the Soviet Union that perfection is an impossible archetype. What we need to do is to focus on being distinctive and becoming the best country that we can be, no matter what the world throws at us.*

There is a natural uneasiness throughout the world about Communism and what our culture has embraced. The only way to alleviate this tension is to re-write Communism. We need to extract the animus of Bolshevism and redefine our history in a way that justifies the direction we are taking.

The people of the Soviet Union long for security above all else. There are indeed a few trouble makers, like the Trotskyites and his Left Opposition, inside and outside our borders for whom the thrill of the unplumbed is an emotional compulsion. But I affirm that the Soviet people, taken as a whole, desire to be free of fear for their future. They need to know that they can depend on me, to frame their lives in advance.

We have a history with shared values and traditions. It is essential that the basic characteristics which tie us together be protected from any threats. Because of this, I must attempt to rid our culture of this threat, even if through the use of distorted or violent means.

Leon Trotsky: Journal

During the Copernican Revolution there was discontent with the Ptolemaic system. Men of intellect were losing faith in the ancient philosophers and there was a need for a new scientific affectivity preferring discipline and simplicity. In order for this to take place, there needed to be a rebellion against the Church. Those who raised the flag of revolution (the scientific elite) became the militant intelligentsia, because of the psychological and social factors involved. The scientific advantages and irreducible political message that took place, when the sun was put at the center of the universe, was clearly enough to draw in the rest of the scientists and writers. It provided a new azimuth for those who were frustrated with the old system of beliefs and credenda.

Joseph Stalin: Journal

I liken the old Bolsheviks with the struggle for writers for existence during the Renaissance. They were made up of a small
group of competitors, playing a very real game of intrigue. They knew
each other extremely well, and found themselves involved in a retic-
ulum of petty jealousy, envy, slander and equivocation. Their clique
transiency was as boundless as the sea, when they all started to fight
with each other. As Aristotle called it: "potter against potter." Envy
appears when other's ideas or achievements become a deliberation on
our own. What they hate most, is when the nature of their failures is
made transparent.

5

Nineteenth century economists envisioned that technological advances and the resulting abundance it would produce, along with the modern organization of the workforce, would create a post-materialistic world. They saw people existing with a higher level of cultural, intellectual, and spiritual cogency. In this world, the significance of economic considerations should have abated. But, we did not witness the end of economics. The Spain I lived in during the civil war was actually a time when economics and its import were more prevalent than ever before. The cycle of hope and disappointment lay at the heart of capitalism.

Spain had indeed discarded the fundamental and inevitable values and standards of a previous era. But now, it had no sense of who it was and how it fitted into the rest of the world. It was shipwrecked on the shore of ambiguity and instability.

We were unhappy. I was unhappy. I felt like the howls of my discontent would convulse the bulwark of the world. The war was amputating one thing after another: the intellect, the will, and the sense of resolution. Spain was baying at the moon and dissolving in its tears.

Just as the modern world is ignorant of man's happiness, so it is also ignorant of its unhappiness.

I could imagine a home that could express my longing for native heath and my desire for leaving it behind. It would be like my mother: that which could both hold me and let me go. I looked to the world now as equal parts — place and journey.

I now found myself in Moscow. My mother had been sent there before me. I was there for Soviet spy training and tradecraft.

The three main primary elements that I studied were: covert residency, source recruiting, and source manipulation. The Academy's Diplomatic Preparation Department taught me about cover duties, through courses in diplomatic etiquette and attaché observation, collection, and reporting. We then moved on to covert tasks, operational and informational reporting, and the organization of deep-cover operations.

I did learn about the organization of foreign armed forces and their intelligence, but deep cover is what turned out to be my future role in the GPU. The plan to get Trotsky was already in the works.

The Special Preparation Department taught me the trade-craft. My focus here was on intelligence history and methodology, organization, techniques (the art of sabotage and kidnapping were particular favorites of ours), Soviet intelligence objectives, procedures under official-cover and under deep-cover, and (most importantly for me) the organization of third-country operations. This included agent recruitment and direction, operational techniques, communications (be it radio or contacting superiors through other methods), photography, secret writing, camouflage and concealment, and counterintelligence evasion.

We were taught that the GPU existed largely to express the Soviets beliefs about the world. It made perfect sense to me, because not unlike philosophy and the sciences, we can only express beliefs about the world, not our knowledge of it. Impressions are the raw material of the world: the colors, shapes, and sounds, and reflections of our emotions and desires.

6

Leon Trotsky: Journal

After the October Revolution, we dissolved the old police and created the Workers and Peasants' Militia under the supervision of the NKVD. They quickly became overwhelmed by functions inherited from the Imperial government, such as supervision of all the local governments, policing, and firefighting. The new proletarian workforce turned out to be too inexperienced. This overtaxing left us with no capable security force, so we created a secret political police — the Cheka. Very soon after this, it gained the right to undertake quick non-judicial trials and executions, if it was deemed necessary to protect the Revolution. It was reorganized in 1922 as the GPU or State Political Directorate of the NKVD. By the time of my exile the NKVD had become a monsterocracy that simultaneously controlled intelligence, the secret police, guarded the frontier, ran concentration camps, and had a large army force. But the GPU had become the private army of Joseph Stalin.

The bloodletters, who are devouring the Revolution by either murdering the old Bolsheviks or driving them to suicide, are mostly terrified and mediocre men who are trained in their methodologies, are disciplined, and are hubristically relentless. The instrument of terror is now in control of the nation even while being terrified itself.

I feel embarrassed because I have always said that police states, torture, and evil handicraft cannot hold a country together, but the NKVD shows evidence to the contrary. Their adulteration of Communism has not yet been confuted. Stalin still rules. The Soviet Union exists as a mafiocracy that is ruthless enough to do anything for the purpose of ascendancy.

With the abuse of power, they have exceeded the legitimate exercise of authority and have imposed their own fantasies, greed, and gluttony on the people.

7

Leonid Eitingon: Journal

We have begun penetrating Trotsky's household on the island of Prinkipo, in Turkey, and the differing groups of the Left Opposition throughout the world. Jakob Frank, the Lithuanian Jew, who has worked at Prikipo for a time, has come over to our side. Another agent, known as Kharin, obtained the text of an edition of Bulletin of the Opposition, which disrupted its output for a short period. Paul Okun has also been very effective as a plant in the Administrative Secretariat of the Left Opposition.

The fact that there are so few Russian Bolshevik–Leninists abroad has made it easy for us to infiltrate their organization. Purely from a technical point of view, it is difficult for them to find sympathizers who speak and write Russian, in order to carry out secretarial duties.

Rudolf Klement, Trotsky's secretary, has been murdered in Paris.

Erwin Wolf, another supporter of Trotsky who had gone to Spain, has been murdered.

Ignace Reiss, a former GPU agent who renounced Stalin and supported the Fourth International, has been murdered in Switzerland.

I have started hatching an idea to infiltrate Trotsky's household for the purpose of assassinating him. I believe that we can use one of our agents to seduce an American Trotskyite, Sylvia Ageloff, as a way in. We have information that she will attend a secret conference of Trotsky's Fourth International in France. One of Ageloff's acquaintances, Ruby Weil, is starting to waver. We believe we can turn her. An agent named Gertrude is in Paris already, who will contact Weil and help her to set up a meeting between Ageloff and Mercader.

I have chosen Ramón Mercader for this assignment. He has showed much growth through his training. At first he did not seem comfortable in his own skin. But with training, he has been able to see how solutions to his problems can appear on the horizon in exact proportion to how he faces what he fears most. For Ramón, this is cruelty. At first, he could not think of anything worse. There is nothing more frightening to many people than this aspect of themselves.

Most young recruits experience this. They have a limited grasp of reality and tend to shy away from the cruelties in the world and flee into the anagogic mode of empathy.

Ramón's beliefs are now in line with ours: beliefs about goals; beliefs about norms; beliefs about oneself; and beliefs about reality.

For my plan to work, I need someone who will be best suited to exploiting a lonely woman. Ramón has experienced consistent exploitation from his overbearing mother. People like this often have developed various complex interpersonal behavior patterns in order to protect themselves. It is a way to feel less fearful and perhaps more important. They have a natural tendency to attract others who are easy to take advantage of. It is a natural skill for them. Subconsciously they are able to develop sophisticated games to exploit other people in ingenious ways. And they do so in such a way that their behavior seems socially acceptable on the surface.

The more negative experiences a person has had, the more they fear relationships. And the more they fear relationships, the more they revert to their rigid interpersonal pathologies to exploit other people. Men like Ramón repeat interpersonal patterns and behaviors across a wide range of situations, because they have developed nihilistic and irreconcilable expectations about the characteristics of other people, along with uncompromising beliefs about the ways in which to behave in these situations.

8

The plan was in effect and I found myself in Paris. My cover was Jacques Mornard. I was a Belgian journalist and my activities were related to writing sports articles. I also had several business interests and a wealthy mother.

After creating a sentimental liaison with Sylvia Ageloff, I would be able to penetrate Trotsky's circle within a short two years.

The entry to Ageloff was — desire. Desire is something we can choose to consciously engage in or ignore. Sylvia had chosen the later. I had to awaken it. What most people do not realize is that we are incapable of disengaging from the erotic. Our inner natures are desire laden. It is embodied in the human character. To get there though, I had to go through the head.

Sylvia was an intellectual, so I had to appeal to the desire of the human spirit first. The inspiration to transcend who we are and what we do is an abiding drive of this spirit. In order to transcend these things one needs to pass beyond their human limitations. For Sylvia, this included social inadequacy issues: fear of looking foolish, losing control, making mistakes, feelings of being rejected by others, failure, being dressed unsuitably, being teased, and ideas of possible homosexuality. I needed to motivate her urge to transcend these things and move beyond their barriers and limitations. For Sylvia many of these limitations were only imagined.

I applied many of the techniques that I had observed Leonid Eitingon use to seduce my mother: using witticism, irony, teasing, and joking. She was full of sarcasm at first, so I needed to break down this propensity. I would mimic her manners and then show her how she could gradually convert sarcasm into novelty and originality. This helped her to overcome the conscious restraints that were initially present in her posture and lessoned her resistance.

As Freud said, wit is a Janus that can develop a thought simultaneously in two opposite directions. When there is a discrepancy in feelings and perceptions, as is the case with humor, the resulting laughter from this discrepancy testifies to the relaxing effect of wit. I wanted her to think that I was a creative person, since the jump from stress to discharge can be quite unexpected and unpredictable. This is the brevity of wit.

As I brought out the defiant power of her frail spirit, she began to develop the tenacious determination needed to deal with life's challenges. This was crucial, because it is this defiant power that enables us to move into relationships we believe in and fancy.

Her defenses weakened. She had kept so much of herself at a safe distance for so long. When somebody does this, they are barely able to ever experience the impelling force of their spirit. Nothing can make a person feel more insecure and unsafe, than trying to maintain that safety.

We eventually made love. I made her feel whole.

To feel whole is to feel organic unity. It is to feel, at least for one brief moment, a totality and familiarity with life. It is to feel concordance with oneself and with others, and to have insight to your place in the larger sense of transcendental essence. It upholds that life is worth living and that loneliness can be surpassed.

Plato said, "Like his father, however, Love is a schemer after the beautiful and the good, an intrepid hunter full of courage, boldness, and hungry for knowledge, he's a confirmed philosopher, a sorcerer and brewer of potions, and a skilled sophist. By nature he's neither mortal nor immortal, but when things go well for him, he'll come to life and flourish in a day, then die, then revive again."

Ageloff was in love with me. I was neither mortal nor immortal. I was the ebb of life, yet I was also the ebb of death: whoever knows the heart, also knows how fragmented, stupid, desolate, and conceited it really is. It is more apt to ruin than it is to save.

When she looked into my eyes, it was as if she held the secret of my being and knew who I really was. But the profound meaning of my being was outside of me, imprisoned in my omissions.

9

Leonid Eitingon: Journal

*M*odern love is nothing more than delusion. It absorbs the thoughts and feelings of those who pretend to be in love, and isolates them from the collective. In the Soviet Union this separation will become pointless. Love is not a private matter involving only the two lovers. It enjoys a uniting element that is valuable to the collective. Throughout history, society has been the one to establish the norms that define when and under what circumstances love is legal, and when love is corrupt.

The experience of love, once it has gone through the stages of certainty, perception, and understanding, will present an historical account of relations between lovers that focuses on one's desire for recognition and the role of the partner in attaining it. The love of one person for another results in a struggle for recognition, at the end of which one will become lord, or master, and the other slave.

Caridad Mercader: Journal

*T*he present and past are things that cannot be fully understood. As a woman, I have strived toward a new and different stationing for myself and my son. For most; this would result in failure and frustration. To understand the present I have had to become aware of what I truly missed in the past, and then become aware of the extent to which I have suffered from what I really missed.

I now have to fully comprehend the current situation. It is essential that I make sense out of this, in order to understand who I am.

I know that Leonid needs me as an asset for the security of the Soviet experiment. I understand that he will use me to influence and perhaps control Ramón. Yet, I also know that I feel a love for him in a way that I thought impossible before.

Not only do I want his love but I also am desirous of his power, his position, and yes, even his penis. The loneliness and emptiness that I have felt in the past, I blame on my father and that idiot who called himself my husband. Their treatment of the women in their lives made us inferior beings, second-class citizens whose virtue had been stolen from us.

Rousseau expressed the conviction that a woman's distinctive feminine qualities, which are assigned to her by nature, has designated a distinct and different function for her in nature and society. A woman's essential function is to please her husband. Then the attraction for the man is whether victory over her is a demurity which yields to potency or just that the will surrenders.

In Spain, the rule has always been to leave this doubt between him and her.

What I want is to become like Leonid. At times, I want to be him and possess the powers that he has. I want to be a man and leave my *womanly ways in the past. This has made me pushy and insensitive, but it is needed for my new mission. Power not only regulates and shapes desires and identities; it also excludes and erases sexual differ- ence. I will willingly substitute force for relevant connection, except with Ramón.*

Not only in the past but in the present, with all of the changes in our common lives and with culture in general, webs of emotional and intellectual practices have surrounded the attraction of the sexes. Love as we know it now is a complex circumstance of the mind and body, no longer rooted to its biological instinct for reproduction. It is in fact in surreptitious contradiction to it. It is now intricately interlaced with passion, friendship, infatuation, mutual compatibility, sympathy and admiration, familiarity, and most important — maternal tenderness.

Society has told me that there is only one concept of gender, which it defines as normal. It is supposed to serve all of us, discounting out vast differences. For me, the only sex which counts is one that is not exclusively masculine. The traditional Spanish ideas can no longer construct and identify me. The notion of who I am is no longer determined by my sex. I will construct my own narrative: love has changed me.

Love changes a woman completely.

If I dare to love, if I dare to be myself, I can shatter the construct in which the world has confined me.

Leonid Eitingon: Journal

Caridad's personage is divided between what she really is and what she imagines she is, and this has been prescribed to her by her upbringing, marriage, class, school, friends, religion, and her lover — me.

Unfortunately for her, the images that she has of a man's sexual and spiritual parts are not things that she can tangibly possess as parts of her own body and incarnation. She will only know them in her mind and in the radius of this relationship. The feigned belief of masculine power, of wisdom and independence, of viraginous insight, live in her as an irresistible fantasy. They are images of her apprehensions of an essential demarcation and disconformities.

I must be sure not to underestimate her though. Women, taken as a brood, are so much degraded by mistaken estimations of female excellence. This artificial weakness, like the bevel of the sword, can produce a propensity to tyrannize and gives birth to craftiness. They learn to play off a puerile façade that lowers esteem, yet also helps create lust in their quarry.

Our relationship will not suffer the delusions of the modern lover. It will follow the course that nature has set out: either friendship or indifference inevitably succeeds love. This ethos seems absolutely to accommodate with the system of government which prevails in the Communist world and the moral world. There is no doubt that passions are the seditionists of action, and open the curiosity; but they will eventually sink back into mere appetites, relapse into personal and momentary gratification, once the spasm is released, and the submerged mind rests in regalement.

Caridad has abandoned herself to love to save herself; but the paradox of this idolatrous aphrodisia is that in trying to save herself she will deny herself irrevocably in the end.

10

ylvia frequently liked to paraphrase Trotsky when she tried to involve me in her politics. I, on the other hand, always maintained that I never had any political convictions whatsoever.

She insisted that Stalin had emerged as the consequential expression of the second chapter of the Revolution. She said that Trotsky called it the "morning after."

"Why would one of the foremost leaders of the Bolshevik Party allow Stalin to consolidate all the power into his hands?" I asked.

"Perhaps his policies were too doctrinaire, I guess," she responded. "His policies were impractical, when he needed to be more pragmatic. In essence, he allowed himself to be out-maneuvered."

"Maybe Stalin was simply more astute," I countered with reservation. I didn't want to appear too interested.

"I have to say, though, that I can't and won't see it as a personal struggle for power between the two," she said. "Trotsky just never imagined that the working class of Russia could survive in global isolation. It is too economically backward and culturally primitive of a country. This is why we are committed to the Fourth International.

"Trotsky calls it the victory of the bureaucracy," she continued, "and says that only idle observers and fools can attribute Stalin's rise to power from any kind of personal forcefulness or exceptional cunning."

"The what?" I asked, feigning infelicity.

"Historical forces — you silly. Am I getting too cerebral for you again?" she said with a laugh.

I rolled over to the nightstand to pull a cigarette out of its package. I lit the Gitanes, took a deep drag and started to cough. For some reason I felt that I should learn how to smoke, now that I was a spy. I put it out. This was a habit that I soon abandoned.

"Maybe so," I replied, "but for now, let's get back to more important things." I switched off the lights and proceeded to lower my head to between her thighs. Her moans were tender and languishing, as long and silent as the velvet darkness.

Martial, the Roman poet, must have foreseen this moment, for her gift to me was, "the fragrance of balsam extracted from aromatic trees; the ripe odor yielded by the teeming saffron; the perfume of fruits mellowing in their winter buds; the flowery meadows in the summer; amber warmed by the hand of a girl; a bouquet of flowers that attracts the bees."

Yes, the soupçon of our congress was all of these…and more.

All of her blood and all of her spirit, melted down to this illicit kiss.

11

Leon Trotsky: Journal

I am still convinced that the workers need to regain power in Russia in order to carry out the unfinished tasks of the Revolution. The workers of the more developed capitalist countries are needed in collaboration. This is simply true, because with socialism, it requires a higher level of production compared to capitalism.

I warned everyone years ago, that the backward nature of a country like Russia would eventually lead to the growth of a bureau-cracy. My protestations of the arbitrary behavior of the Party crystallizing under Stalin were going to be irreversible. Even Lenin agreed with me on this point.

The Comintern is nothing but a Babylonian structure, standing as a bleached shell, both ideologically and politically. It is the Left Opposition who now stand as the true Marxist—Leninist revolution-aries. Our cadres, which are not yet a legion, are nonetheless indefatigable.

Trotsky was beginning to draw together the nucleus of a group of genuine Bolsheviks. It was up to men like me to ferociously attempt to destroy everything he was working for. News came to me that Trotsky's daughter, Zinaida, had been driven to suicide in Berlin. Her husband, Planton Volkov, was arrested and was never heard from again. Alexandra Sokolovskaya had been sent to a concentration camp. She was Trotsky's first wife and I had heard that it was she who had introduced Trotsky to socialist ideas in the first place. Another son of Trotsky, Sergey, had been arrested on charges of "poisoning the workers." He was a scientist with no political interests or connections. He was simply the son of Stalin's enemy. Trotsky's small apparat was being dismantled. We were sending Lev Davidovich Bronstein, the Jew who had taken the name Leon Trotsky, a message.

We were engaged in a systematic and bloody terror directed at a whole generation of Bolshevik-Leninists. We would bury the ideas and the personality of Trotsky under a profusion of lies, misintelligence of history, slanders, and fabrications.

What some of Stalin's critics said may have been true, but they were policies driven out of necessity. Some of the blunders of the Stalin–Bukharin leadership, during the defeat of the German Revolution in 1923, reinforced the retreat of the New Economic Policy. The consequence of this was that it sped up the formation of a bureaucratic caste, which put itself before the interests of the international revolution. But when you look back at it, this revolution was not in the interests of Russia. Stalin's actions were reflecting the interests of bureaucracy — the system that was working.

This is why it was necessary to make Trotsky an ideological bogey. What the Soviet Union did not need was a program for the restoration of a worker's democracy that could possibly find momentum among the new younger workers. Any possibility of a struggle against bureaucratic degeneration meant that there was no other solution than a bloody purge against the Opposition.

As a Spaniard, I was not playing a small part. During the civil war, the Soviet regime instigated a propaganda campaign back in Russia. They sought to underline the parallels between the Russian civil war and the conflict in Spain; the goal being to portray the Spanish Nationalists as an international fascist conspiracy. The Kremlin provided state-run radio and newspapers with complete coverage of the civil war, along with reactions. Three thousand Spanish orphans were evacuated to the Soviet Union in 1937. In Russia they lived in relative comfort and security and displayed to the people Stalin's bigheartedness. When I trained in Moscow, my ethnicity was not an encumbrance.

In fact there were others like me, because the Kremlin's policy at the time was infiltrate, penetrate, and hope for an opening. Most were sent back to Spain, to gather intelligence on the nature of Spanish politics, society, and culture. Key operations included cementing ties with potential collaborators. But I ended up here in Paris. My fate would be different from my fellow Spaniards.

12

Joseph Stalin: Journal

*T*he unfulfilled tend to be injustice collectors.
As for myself, I delight in another's failures or defeats.
Nothing brings this out more for me than the spectacle of the mighty fallen, especially if they are the naturally bright — I love to see them founder.

Ideologues like Trotsky try to come to power by pledging an envy-free society. People like this labor to bridal the disintegrative forces of rivalry for their own purposes. Of course their goals will only come to disaster, because they ignore the psychic reality of envy: it can never be cast out, any more by a government than by an ideology. Envy always returns from rhetorical exile — with all the sweet revenge of the cabined, cribbed, and confined.

The Bolshevik–Leninist faith preaches an unenvying posture among persons. It is like the New Testament of the Orthodox priests:

love and grace will come to all, regardless of talent, degree of cognizance or intellect, class, race, or sex. But what they don't realize is that all of these distinctions are exactly what makes envy. Religion fails, namely when parity of access to God's grace and love becomes translated into a mission to manufacture their egalitarian society, solely based on guilt. As with all new freedoms, it eventually falls victim to the perverting powers; where it becomes the fault of the envied ones that the enviers envy them. This proves that the envied, be it religious or Communist, have failed in their mission to make all equal on earth because if all people are to be equal before God and society, they must also be equal in every other way, including talent and position in society.

This is the mistake of the Opposition: all of the shortcomings and historical retrenchments of their social philosophy and economic theory, have depended on the assumption that human envy is the outcome of peremptory, unorganized, and temporary circumstances. They believe that it can be cured, once the gross inequalities are removed.

I have found that when you use envy as the fulcrum of social policy, it is much more destructive than what the old Bolsheviks, who have fabricated their philosophy on this principle, would ever admit.

Leon Trotsky: Journal

Our feelings about things are intermingled with our beliefs about them. Whether these beliefs can be adapted from different situations or state of affairs depends on if they are able to represent practical solutions. However, in the case of Stalin, his erroneous and negative beliefs about eclectic injustice and inferiority have figured in the maintenance and etiology of his criminal syndicalism.

For him, the doctrine of Marxism includes a plan of revenge for the envious. It is in the abstract and ennobled concept of the proletariat, the dispossessed, and exploited, where he finds his position of implacable envy to be legitimized.

Envy becomes political when it becomes common. It becomes nebulous when the large bureaucracy feels more favored for the kinds of goods they possess than for the defining objects themselves.

The truth is that it is collectively disadvantageous; those who envy others are prepared to do things that make both the worse for wear.

This is the man who leads the Communist Party in Russia: the unholy dread of what ought to be is at the very marrow of his tellurian evil. The mystery of evil itself lies in this idiosyncrasy. Those who occupy this echelon stand not just against goodness but are egregiously opposed to those who are deserving. They are unnerved by life itself. They fear it as much as the grave itself. What their envy hungers after is the death of others.

Since the time of Augustine, many have proclaimed evil as the privation of being, yet it is here and it exists. It is more alive in its denials than other things are in their affirmations. Hatred and envy have confronted themselves in Russia, and are competing among themselves for power. The effect has been an about-face of values and a methodical corruption and reinterpretation of the Communist manifesto, where what was evil now appears to be good.

13

ylvia and I were taking a stroll by the Cathedral of Notre Dame. She was talking, but I did not hear her, as I stopped to gaze at the tall structure. An overwhelming sense of catharsis came to me, which was the basis for my aesthetic reaction. The horror of death was completely obliterated by the Dionysiac triumph of the poetico-mystical lines. I was struck by the contrast between material and form. The refractoriness of the stone is the greatest challenge to the creation of such structures. I thought it remarkable how the architect could force the stone to take on this shape, to sprout branches, so the material magnitude could reach its zenith, the whole edifice straining heavenward with tremendous dynamism, yet also seeming ready to float away. I could see boldness and courage. I could sense the effect of an arrow shot into the sky.

Death is not a terrorist or hobgoblin. It is no wonder the master placed those ugly and horrifying gargoyles atop. Without them the cathedral would be unimaginable. The story of this configuration contained a hidden meaning. The building's trajectory which seemed to lead to happiness could lead to misery as well, displaying the interplay of these two directions.

"Why haven't you gone to any sporting events, dear?" she asked, as my focus returned to her.

"What?"

"You know. You haven't mentioned attending any sporting events."

I hesitated for a moment. "Those trips that I have been taking, well those were actually to football matches, and not the type of business trips that you might have thought I was going on."

"But you were the one who told me they were business trips having to do with your mother's affairs," she countered.

"Did I?"

"Yes."

"Well, they were actually both."

My stories about my trips were becoming conflicting and more preposterous as time had passed between us, but I wasn't too concerned really. When I look back at it, I guess that I was lucky, because trust is one of the first things to go and one of the last things to return in a relationship. When it does return, it has to overcome fantasies that life is in our control, and often we feel at fault when it is not. At least I acknowledged its unfolding with a sense of compassion for Sylvia, who was trembling at the thought of what would come next, whether tragedy or grace.

"Let me ask you this, Jacques: can I meet your parents? I'm assuming that we are a couple, and I want them to meet me."

"Sylvia, this is hard for me to say, but I know that they won't accept you. They have old European, aristocratic ways. I don't believe that someone from your station in America will be acceptable to them. Please don't let this upset you. We are different here in Europe. All you need to know is that I love you."

She swallowed this story with reservations; she was blinded by love.

Sylvia took my hands and looked straight into my eyes.

"Jacques, my happiness with you has been like a tapestry of many colors, and what makes this tapestry a picture of rapture is not the overmeasure of bright colors, but the contrast between darkness and light. You have given me a sense of hope and joy when I was in the midst of sorrow. Remember what Hamlet said, 'When sorrows come, they come not like single spies, but in battalions.' With you, all of these are forgotten."

I soon learned that Sylvia was to return home. In February of 1939 I informed her that I had accepted a position in New York as a correspondent for a Belgian newspaper and would be following her there in just a few weeks.

It wasn't until September that I arrived. I was called back to Moscow, in the meantime, for debriefing. I arrived finally in New York with a forged Canadian passport. The NKVD forger had misspelled the name, so I was now known to immigration as Frank Jacson.

Sylvia Ageloff: Journal

Jacques has come to New York many months after he said he would. When we met at the Oak Room he was wearing his familiar princely smile. He even seemed to joke about his untimely arrival, but our meeting was almost business-like.

I am beginning to harbor some leeriness about his erraticism and odd affectations. Those who are truly in love act with confidence, straightforwardness, and honesty. Those who just present themselves as nice are often only hiding the subterraneity of their sadness, behind a show of smiling appeasement.

More so than ever, he has the tendency to put on the facial expressions, voices, postures, and movements of the people around him. This mirroring starts to get awkward now that I have become conscious of it. His mimicking of me, in particular, gives me the uncomfortable sensation that I am being manipulated. This behavior that started on the surface is now starting to reverberate at the deepest emotional level. For Jacques, this mirroring seems to be as natural, and as subconscious, as breathing itself.

What I don't understand, is that he is somehow different from when we were together in Paris. At one moment, he can take something as an insult, and at another time take the same thing as a joke. What will at one time excite anger; will at another time hardly be noticed.

I guess all I can do is to attribute this to his European eccentricities.

When I get upset, I find it useful to remind myself that whatever is bothering me is usually not anything as serious as I may think. My problems only seem serious because I am making unnecessary associations in my mind. When I get highly emotional, I need to take some time out and distance myself from the situation to calm down.

Now that Jacques is back in my life, I find it hard to find this distance.

Whenever I make overtures to this effect, Jacques seems to send me subtle messages in order to control me and indicate that he is the one with dominion over me.

Unconscious realizations have the ability to distract our decisions when we are not even aware of their intrusions. Painful experiences act in this manner. They can be consciously eliminated, though, and I have started substituting many of my former phobias that were familiar to me, and now they do not feel as painful.

At the same time, I realize that almost all of the things that are upsetting me are small and unimportant. I just needed to put this all on paper. The reason I get so distressed about so many things lies in the fact that I am associating small problems with more profound problems, which many times are only remotely related to what I'm making such a fuss about. The thing I need to focus on the most is when our bodies are interlaced in coital synergism.

14

I am sure that there were other plans in motion to get Trotsky, that I was not informed of, but what I needed to do was to stick with Sylvia and wait for an opening.

All the while, Stalin had set into motion a plan to eliminate every remnant of opposition to his regime within the Soviet Union. He started, what later would be referred to as the Moscow Trials that sent the leading personalities of the Bolshevik Party to court. They were the vanguard of the proletariat. The prosecution accused them of serving foreign powers and conspiring against the USSR. Trotsky's name was constantly mentioned in all of the confessions. In this way he was presented as the organizer of this conspiracy. The trials even exposed him as an ally of the German secret police and the Japanese empire.

Trotsky was living in Norway at this time. The Soviet Union threatened a boycott of Norwegian trade, if they did not order a domiciliary arrest. They capitulated, and in addition, denied him the right to write about any current political issues or be interviewed by the press. This led to three months of isolation. Even his correspondence was subject to censorship. The socialist Norwegian government started procedures to expel him from the country, but no other country would have him.

There were a group of Mexicans in the International Communist League who had identified themselves with Trotsky and heard that his life was in great danger. They set out to find a place for him on Mexican land.

The famous artist Diego Rivera and professor Octavio Fernandez interceded before President Lázaro Cárdenas to provide political asylum. Shortly after this, Cárdenas ordered that Trotsky be allowed to come to Mexico as a political refugee.

Leon Trotsky, second wife Natalia Sedova, and a handful of close collaborators, soon arrived in the port of Tampico. In a marked contrast to receptions elsewhere, he was given a flamboyant official welcome. His party was given transit to Mexico City in the President's personal train.

Trotsky's arrival coincided with a second Moscow Trial. Natalia used to talk about how they would listen to it on the radio. She would even reminisce, "Lev and I opened the newspapers and our mail, and we could feel the insanity, absurdity, and outrage, fraud and blood were flooding us from all sides."

They ended up in the country suburb of Coyoacan, in a house which was the property of the father of artist Freda Kahlo, Diego Rivera's wife. It was known as the "Blue House," because of its façade.

For security reasons, the windows overlooking the street were walled in with adobe bricks. A garrison of police and personal guards, who were Mexican Trotskyites, acted as custodians of the front entrance.

One of Trotsky's first activities in his new country was to organize his defense against all the accusations that were coming from Moscow. Trotsky set up a counter trial to defend himself against the charges of the real trials. They called it the Preliminary Commission of Inquiry, chaired by the American philosopher and university president John Dewey. It was held in the main hall of Frida Kahlo's house. Here Trotsky made a fool of himself, as he attempted to demonstrate the falseness of all charges against him. The trial was supposed to be composed of impartial people with absolute integrity. After thirteen long days, with the presentation of eighteen accusations and decisive answers, the Dewey Commission turned out to be collaborators by publishing its verdict concluding that the trials in Moscow were judicial frauds. It denounced them before humanity. Trotsky was innocent of all charges. They characterized the Moscow trials as the most "monstrous falsification" in the whole of history.

Leon Trotsky: Journal

Natalia and I find ourselves in a spacious and colorful house, here in Mexico. I am isolated from the rest of the world though. My office is a sanctuary, but in many ways represents an internment. I have my writing, my garden, and my rabbits to occupy my time. I continue my theoretical and literary activities. I am working on a book named, "Stalin's Crimes," which will unmask the Moscow trials. Also, "Their Morals and Ours," which reveals the moral opposing the bourgeois concept of moral, is in the works.

I have had to confront scathing attacks and infamies coming from the Mexican Communist Party and Confederation, which is most definitely a Stalinist controlled organization. They accuse me of being a fascist agent, and even of organizing a foreign counterrevolutionary intervention in Mexico. All are absurd.

I have become the Lady of Shalott. In Tennyson's poem, he contrasts the world outside with the solitude within the Lady's room. Although she may seem content, her admissions prove that she is not. Her discontent will create fateful actions. We will only see, in my case.

In my lucubration, I have begun to search my heart. What I wonder is: can this lead to an itinerary of peace — which will allow me to settle unfinished business?

While in Mexico, Trotsky received news that his son, Leon Sedov, had been poisoned by our agents in a Paris hospital while recovering from an appendix surgery. His youngest son, Sergei Sedov, had been arrested and executed back in Russia.

15

The poet André Breton had gone to Mexico with his companion Jacqueline Lamba, and met with Trotsky. The result of their conversations resulted in a manifesto, "For an Independent Revolutionary Art," which promoted the creation of an international organization of artists, The International Federation of Independent Revolutionary Art.

We had our own sympathizers in the Mexican art community. David Alfaro Siqueiros was one of them, a confirmed Stalinist. No individual can be recognized in Mexico, associated with the arts, who was more involved in direct political action. He was a student agitator and soldier, and considered one of the greatest artistic masters of this century. He held the same regard as Diego Rivera and José Clemente Orozco. He was creative and innovative, interested in new techniques and materials. Most important of all, was that he would advance Stalin's appetence in this part of the world.

In 1936, Siqueiros went to Spain to enlist in the antifascist forces. He served three years. I never met him, but I was aware of who he was. The International Brigades in Spain were notorious recruiting grounds of Stalin's agents and killers, as my story will testify to. There were suspicions of Siqueiros having connections with the GPU. He had spent some time in the Soviet Union in 1928.

David Alfaro Siqueiros: Journal

*C*he most cheerful fact in man's history is that the presentation of sadness in art can give pleasure to people. This means that grief is closer to happiness than man has provisionally accepted. Tragedy has historically been enjoyed. We listen with keen pleasure to music that is sad. To me, this is the most hopeful thing in the world.

Art holds the decipherment to the questions of our lives, because in it, the antipodal points which can confuse us are made conspiratorial.

This is life's miserly, tenuous thread: living things can at any moment become non-living; death is just an asthmatic wheeze away. The contexture we depend on for meaning and safety is in fact capricious and weak.

I am starting to experiment with materials and innovative tools that I believe are essential for creating a modern revolutionary art, using an airbrush and stencils, along with the use of pyroxylin. The works become shiny and inflexible. It does not seem to create any problems for my larger works on composition board, but the smaller ones on paper are much more fragile.

Some of the newer works like FIRE and THE SOB are acknowledging the advance of fascism in Europe and Asia, through subtle metaphor. As Octavio Paz stated in his essay, "The Sons of Malinche," — "The European considers Mexico to be a country on the margin of universal history and everything that is distant from the center of his society strikes him as strange and impenetrable." Yet, through my work, the polemic issues and ideas of this decade are unsheathing themselves here in the new world.

In THE SOB, I have externalized the miserable conditions of life, where the vision of the possibility of better things makes the present misery more intolerable. It can hasten on those who suffer to the struggles, which can improve their lot. But if these struggles only expeditiously results in worsened misery, the outcome can only be unabbreviated desperation. The Mexican, in such a plight, and those who are by no means the least social or insensitive, will rise to violence. Mexico was one of the few countries that underwent a social revolution earlier in the century. Our violence is social and not anti-social.

By striking when and how we can, we are striking not for ourselves, but for humankind; indignant and condemned.

Anger in a modified form has always been the theme of the poet and the artist. When sublimated into nimbler intellectual and willed action, its effect is no less angry though is it less intense. When the artist reacts to and works anger into his work, he is working in accord with the evolutionary function of the emotion — which is to intensify action in a needed direction.

As for passion, it is not an affectivity attached to any single goal but a pervasive, immutable desire independent of any person, thing, or place. The artist must learn at great cost not to control it, for that is impossible — he must reconnoiter it so that it does not destroy him. Passion is an appetite that exceeds the accepted bounds of social code and moral convention.

The congeries of the ordinary is in itself exceptional art.

16

eonid Eitingon was now in New York also. He was the mastermind behind our plot to kill Trotsky and was directing it from the Soviet consulate.

Sylvia had access to Trotsky's inner sanctum and it was my mission to exploit this. In many ways a personal mission is a passionate resolution to bring about a conceivable and future eventuality. You have to be willing to make decisions, act on the propositional function of them, and remain committed until they become irreducible and stubborn reality. If you care about something enough, you commit your instincts to this passion. We were in a life-and-death struggle for the salvation of our grand experiment.

I was to find out later that Leonid had secured the services of David Alfaro Siqueiros three months before my successful attack. Siqueiros had been working in America, mostly in Los Angeles. It was here that he became infatuated with the movies.

I mention this now, because it plays a part in this story. It influenced his use of montage in his murals, along with the use of photography, cinematography, and the use of an air-brush or mechanical brush. His painting confronted the alien influences of other aesthetic expressions, especially the cinema.

He came to Los Angeles to teach muralism at the Chouinard Institute. Ironically, this was the training ground for many of the Disney artists, the icons of capitalism. He became the darling of the film industry. Personalities, such as Tyrone Power, Ira Gershwin, and Charles Laughton, commissioned works from him.

The rumor was that when in New York, he was teaching the union of technique and materials — the impastos, glazing, the use of the spatula, and the painting surface itself, so it could reveal the prophetic vision of the artist — to a young Jackson Pollock.

Siqueiros was a Latin American buccaneer, of paint brush, revolution, and gangsterism.

My mother had arrived in New York and I was to meet her and Eitingon for drinks at Maisonette in the St. Regis. When I walked in, I noticed Siquieros at the bar talking with the American author Ernest Hemmingway. Their continence was jovial; perhaps they were recounting war stories from the International Brigades. I recognized both of them from the newspapers.

Eitingon never led on that he knew either. Our reunion went well. It was nice to see mother, though she looked a little worse for wear. Lines were appearing around her eyes. She was still as beautiful as ever, though. It was here that I was informed that I needed to encourage Sylvia to go to Mexico City. I would follow her under false pretenses and use her to get into the Trotsky compound.

With everything coming into play, I started to experience certain symptoms of anxiety.

Eitingon ended our rendezvous with words of encouragement.

"Ramón, look around you. What do you see? Everywhere that civilization has gone there have been vast improvements in material conditions. And yet men have never been so discontented. It may seem, in view of the amelioration of these conditions, that it appears unreasonable and illogical. But, it will seem less so when you reflect that human nature is unchanged, and that what really needs to be satisfied in this world is the mind and not materiality."

Leonid Eitingon: Journal

What I will need to do with Gnome (Ramón), is to instill in him a motivational disposition to respond in line with the fear and anxiety that he is about to confront. In Mexico, Gnome will come face to face with many rational fears. As a trained agent he should have a good grasp of reality and will deal with the situation. I feel the need for a little bit of insurance, though. If he starts to waver, I will use his mother as an incentive. I will tell him that we are going to kill her if he doesn't complete his task. I will wait until I have no other choice.

It is true that sometimes in the field the core beliefs of agents can become identified and challenged. This can be a problem, because they are often reluctant to change their minds after the turnabout. Remember: emotions and beliefs are clearly intertwined.

When there is a sufficient support system in place, of relevant beliefs, it streams naturally without obstacles or effort. This is when behaviors do not result because of conscious decisions, a weighing of pros and cons in a rational manner. Behaviors can be the product of an integration of different meanings and beliefs that happen without a voluntary or conscious control of the individual. This is addressed in training, but things can happen in the field.

For this reason I have several games in play. I will also have to go to Mexico, to keep Gnome on track.

"Sylvia, I have business in Mexico. I will be there for an extended period."

"Oh! When did this come about? You never mentioned anything about Mexico before," she replied.

"It came up all of a sudden. Some of my business interests in Belgium have developed interests in manufacturing there. It's all really boring business stuff, dear. There is nothing for you to concern yourself with." I only spoke of my cover activities in generic terms, with vague semblance.

"But, what about us? What will happen to me? This is so sudden."

"Sylvia, I have an idea. You have friends in Mexico City. That Trotsky fellow who you talk about all the time is there isn't he? Well just consider, what if you came with me? You could work for him. I mean, you have worked for him in the past, right?"

"Well, yes I have," she said.

"There you have it. Contact whomever you have to and tell them you are coming. Isn't your sister Ruth working for him now? You do want to be near me, don't you? I love you so much that having you there with me in Mexico would mean the world to me."

"I have to think about this, Jacques."

"I think that it is time that I got to know your friends better, dear. You mean so much to me. I have to admit something to you." I looked her in the eyes and softly said, "There are selfish reasons that I want you to come with me, Sylvia. Being in that backwards country, having you in my bed at night will help save me from the loneliness that awaits me there. The smell of you, the sensations of your soft skin, the moans of ecstasy you whisper in my ear when we are making love — things that I can not live without."

I had no reservations about exploiting her. People are constantly fighting their fear of being exploited. It is referred to as "fighting your demons." I do not see the demon in myself; I see it in others. I blame my fears on other people, and I retaliate by exploiting others.

17

Joseph Stalin: Journal

expect to emerge from this decade with the Trotskyite opposition purged and with a detailed political project in place, the contours and content of which will no longer be questioned by anyone. My program of forced collectivization and industrialization will be unquestioned and the bureaucracy will have consolidated power from the working classes.

For every leader who appears in one of the Moscow Trials, hundreds or thousands will be silently imprisoned, and sent to certain death in our Arctic camps, if not summarily executed in their cells. If I must — millions will rot because of their obstinacy. They can howl and thunder their rebellion from the top of their voices in the freezing wastelands.

For those who were members of the military secretariat or who were on Trotsky's armed train during the civil war, envy has led to an *inescapable and unappeasable complexion. Their campaign has induced these begrudging men to constantly react to the political environment, in Russia, in such a way that their envy can not be assuaged. They will fail, because it is utterly hopeless to strive for a society that is free of rivalry by social reform.*

So long as I keep balance in our society, where envy finds expression and recognition in a way that is legitimate and functions within the framework of the Soviet culture and its technology, neither the society's efficiency nor the opportunities of our more ingenious members will be restricted. If, however, the division between private envy and sanctioned envy is not well defined by the government, individual actions and coalitional movements may occur with consequences that would be unfortunate for the Soviet experiment engineered by the bureaucracy, indeed.

In our society, this Soviet controlled touchstone; the worker is not so much concerned with the amount of his wage as with recognition of the difference between him and other workers. This will increase production and the economy will burst with health.

I admit that envy is unyielding and irreconcilable. It is exacerbated by the slightest differences, which can be witnessed in any family. It provides a dynamic for social revolution, but I am convinced that it cannot of itself develop any sort of well-defined revolutionary program.

What will preserve this new government from anarchic resentment is not the assizement of current equality achieved. It will be through our institutions and the inherited objectives of brutal facts, which will make fast the awareness of our limitations in regards to mutual comparisons. And this will ensure collective peace.

18

Leon Eitingon: Journal

*G*oethe wrote: "With most of us the requisite intensity of passion is not forthcoming without an element of resentment, and common sense. And careful observation will, I believe, confirm the opinion that few people who amount to anything are without a good capacity for hostile feelings upon which they draw freely when they need it."

Caridad has a secret. She thirsts for power, but at the same time has a deep need to experience mortification. There is a club, down a dark alley, in the heart of New York's downtown district. In it the sexual proclivities of people like Caridad are practiced. She has exposed her naked body to a small audience of connoisseurs. A man in a mask produces a series of ropes that are used to bind her into submission. My operative, David Alfaro Siqueiros is there. David is sketching her as she lowers her head and submits to what comes next. He says that he will be putting this into a painting later. He says that he will call the work, "Victima Proletaria." The painter's artistic concentration may have been focused on the polemic metaphor, but when he stops sketching and forces himself on her, he was evincing nothing more than Adamic salacity.

I have another agent there, who is taking photographs with a miniature camera. I may need these in the future. They graphically depict Caridad bound and naked.

Nature will either deliver us from the despoliation it imposes on us, or enlighten us how to endure it. What nature will not do is tell us anything about the abominations that come from ourselves. We are relinquished to ourselves. As victims of our own purgatorial fires, we succumb to our gratifying lamentations and extol ourselves, with tears that should have left us blushing.

This painting should hang in the Hermitage.

19

The authentic self is not the same as the one who is apparent in the superficial world. The intimate self, though unhewn and embryonic, is more estimable and authentic than the public presentation.

I was so glad that my mother was there in New York. Just knowing that she was looking out for me was reassuring. Only I knew the real Caridad. Her handlers perhaps could only perceive a varnish of external urbanity. But she was more astute at conferring a certain grace or pliancy in the management of her illusiveness than they could even imagine.

They would find out that even politics, a science in which men are particularly envious, it is not beyond the reach of the enterprising and audacious female. What Caridad knew full well is that, because there are restraints on the employment of female genius, she had to be more inclined toward genuine confidence than to demurity, yet also limit the display of her real talents and predilections.

My mother had me read Shakespeare as a boy. I now can see that she had fastened upon the traits of Shakespeare's strongest females.

Like Miranda, her simplicity was most striking. There was a domestication of disposition — compassionate undercurrents, which were unrestrained by intuition.

Like Isabella, she was reproachless, urbane, and devoted. Her intellectual efficacy was respected; in argument and persuasion alike. She did not offend by gender: her phallicisms being mitigated and coupled with the eternal feminine.

Like Beatrice, her wit could testify to her resentments. She employed it as defense and covert mystification; concealing her thoughtful obstinacy through the subterfuge of impetuosity.

Like Portia, she was observant, perceiving, and subtle; never betraying any reticent arousal.

And like Cordelia, she had a sensibility that was presided over by reason and suitability. Sorrow and resentment was her coxswain. There was a reluctant languishment in her allure.

Caridad Mercader: Journal

he validation of a woman by a man occurs only after she has validated herself as a composite ego, male and female. She must be able to appreciate herself in superiority as well as in doglike devotion and compliance. In order for her to have risen above her Faustianism, she will have rebelled and challenged the conventions of the society or her community. To most, the fight is lost before it ever started. The forces and standards of conventionality extinguish any attempt to shake off the yoke.

The bonds of companionship should be respected, provided that they remain serviceable to us. One should never love another person, except for selfish reasons. They must be forgotten when we can no longer obtain anything from them; to love others for themselves is fond illusion. Nature never inspires in us anything more than that which should prove useful to us. This is the egoist ethos of Nature. Nothing has a larger ego than Nature; then let us be egoists too, if we are to appropriate her edicts.

This revelation has come to me here in New York. My blind devotedness to Leonid has undergone a metamorphosis — all through the pragmatism of amatory discipline; a recognition of necessity.

When you consider Proletarian Morality: it combines equality in relationships, comradely sensitivity, and mutual recognition. The bourgeois culture encouraged the sense of property, where one owned the heart and soul of the other person. We on the other hand recognize the rights of the loved one. We exhibit the ability to listen and understand the mind's core of the beloved. Here we find the end to male selfishness and the suppression of the female anima.

The bedazzling and exacting passions will weaken, along with the sense of property. The complacency of the masculine and the self-

yielding of the woman shall come to an end. Now the true and worthwhile elements of love will develop. The rights of another's personality will be respected, and a communistic sensitivity will be learned: love will not only be expressed through caressing and sexual union but also in joint creativity and activity.

20

In the beginning of 1939, because of political differences, Trotsky and Diego Rivera ended their relationship. Because of this Trotsky felt he should move from the Blue House. His secretary, translator, and bodyguard, Jean van Heijenoort, found an unoccupied house that was being rented and met all of Trotsky's requirements. It had many rooms, a large garden, and was enclosed by a wall. After remodeling, the party moved in to the new house located on Avenida Viena.

The neighborhood was a residential area with rustic scenery. The street names were adopted from European cities, and heroes of the Mexican independence. The house was at the end of a street, and stood along the Churubusco's riverbank. It belonged to the Turati family, a merchant family. Built in 1903, the large house was for a long time, a recreational villa. Inside the walls of the villa, the compound was made of two buildings. To the north was a watchtower, topped with a metal eagle. There was a large lawn and a garden where Trotsky could keep his rabbits. To the south was a one-floor house shaped as a T, with many rooms and surrounded by a large porch. The house was topped with a balustrade with huge flowers made of marble paste.

It was in ruined condition when van Heijenoort found it. Even some of the floors had given way. So a series of repairs were made before the party could move in. Fortification works were of utmost importance. They closed the main entrance and the balcony overlooking the Avenida. The wall was raised and a new entrance door that was more secure was installed. In addition to all this a two-floor brick building was built next to the wall nearest the river. This was to be used to house the security guards. Later, a sophisticated alarm system was installed, with an electronic device to open the front door.

Most of neighboring houses were made of adobe and scattered amongst corn fields and leafy eucalyptus trees.

The rabbit hutches were in the garden. It was part of Trotsky's daily routine to care for them himself. He was quite scientific in their keep, formulating the diet and cleaning the cages. The garden was the area in which everything was developed around. He planted cactus, his preeminent hobby, among areas of grass surrounded by flowering huts. He planted tall, leafy trees, as well as daisies, lilies, plantains, and climbing roses.

In the main building was Trotsky's suite: study, two bedrooms, a bathroom and family dressing room. Also in the main building were the kitchen, the dining room and another office for the secretaries and bodyguards.

In the north wing were rooms for the guards, a storage room, a henhouse, and just outside were the rabbit hutches.

Outside of the compound was an escort of five policemen lead by Jesús Rodriguez Casas. At the end of the street a booth was installed for these officers. Inside of the house there were always around eight to ten Trotskyites to keep guard.

The entourage had two automobiles: a Ford and a Dodge.

*T*hroughout the history of postcolonial Mexico there has been a struggle to acquire nationhood, in spite of the obstacles of diverse ethnicity and race, language, culture, and its geographic isolation. Mexico's sense of nationalism comes from the necessity of unifying many diverse cultural groups in a struggle against foreign domination.

All of the emerging political movements have been a response to outside forces rather than internal ones. The national conscious and cultural integration has progressively increased with a distinctly anti-foreign attitude. They are recovering from a long history of over three hundred years of oppression.

The Revolution of 1910 destroyed the feudalistic reign of Porfirio Díaz and established a new social order based on the principles of democracy. It was followed by a bloody period: ten years of the majority of presidents assasinated, as well as around half a million other Mexicans.

When a leftist government came into power in 1920, a period of relative stability followed. President Alvaro Obregón brought important reforms: the feudal hacienda system eliminated; labor organized and reformed; education declared free and secular; health and welfare programs instituted; as well as programs for the indigenous culture. Two years after this the Mexican Communist Party was founded.

Soviet agents had begun infiltrating Mexico in 1918 with the intent of perfusing the Mexican Socialist Party, bringing with them an immediate diffusion of Communist cultural propaganda. In 1920, the Soviet Union officially recognized the Mexican Communist Party.

The agenda of the Soviet Union was to undermine the Mexican Revolution. We suggested pre-conquest culture as nationalistic symbols. For our instigators, a new nationalism could be used as a weapon of political and cultural warfare designed to alienate Latin America from the United States. Their aim was to sow discord and create confusion in the Mexican psyche. Latin American intellectuals were recruited as co-conspirators to propagate these ideas. Anything that tended to unite Latin Americans with one another and with the United States and Europe was disparaged. Artists, in particular, played a large role through their use of symbolism and motifs, from pre-conquest Indian culture, in art, music, literature and film; all in the hopes of changing public thinking.

The artist's powerful nationalistic sentiments did help to initiate a nationalistic movement in the arts, but was unable to undermine the Revolution. The flagrant attempts of the Soviets Communists under the direction of a foreign government only aroused the suspicion of the Mexican workforce.

By the time I arrived, the Mexican Communist Party was completely Stalinist. Its membership had climbed to nearly forty thousand.

They lent support, along with the government to the pro-Soviet republican forces in the Spanish civil war, and provided asylum to tens of thousands of refugees in this conflict.

There were other reasons for us to infiltrate Mexico. The Soviet Union regarded Mexico as a strategic prize. The US–Mexico border is 1,987 miles long, largely unprotected, and would secure for us an American flank. Up to this point, the United States had been able to conduct its foreign policy without worrying about any border threats. If we could desta-bilize the government and establish a foothold in Mexico, we would gain major advantages, with the United States being severely affected. The Gulf of Mexico and the Caribbean Sea lanes would have to be protected as well as the border. They would have to devote considerable funds and military resources to guard its southern frontier.

Leon Trotsky: Journal

Since my arrival here in Mexico, the official Stalinist press and Stalinist-controlled press have carried out a campaign against me. They cry for my immediate expulsion from the country, as "an enemy against Mexico."

Of the things I have been accused of are: representing the government appropriation of the oil companies; organizing a general strike against the Cardenas government; having connections with General Saturnino Cedillo and his armed peasant uprising; being an agent of Nazi Germany; and conspiring with the American FBI against the Mexican Communist Party.

President Cardenas has intervened through an interview granted to La Prensa newspaper, characterizing me as being a man of honor who has scrupulously kept his promise not to intervene in Mexican politics.

I believe that all of these charges point to a coming attempt to assassinate me. The Stalinist press has responded with scurrility, saying that I have a "persecution mania." But the slogan of the Communist Party is, "Death to Trotsky," alleging "interference" in Mexican politics.

I have found that Mexico is not so unlike the rest of the world. During the 1920s and 1930s we have witnessed a transitional period, where the world as we know it today came into being. We have seen a transformation from a pioneer society to a modern one in numerous parts of the globe. In many of these places the transformation has not been easy, or come without a cost, as they have struggled to come to terms with the change. Here in Mexico, as with other countries, the old values were no longer able to provide an adequate ideational frame for their lives. Many have been reluctant to accept this change, and hold onto their old beliefs and values. What we all have in common though, is that it is natural to attempt to retain a sense of stability and order in such a chaotic climate.

In Mexico, the population's expectations of their government tend to be very high. The problem I foresee is that the government's available resources to meet these expectations are low, especially because it is a non-industrialized country. This has, in the past, demonstrated how incumbents in Latin America lose support quickly and tend to lose elections more frequently than in industrialized countries. Hence, electoral behavior becomes based on performance and personality.

For this reason, I have to put faith in Cardenas' personality to hold Mexico together. If he is assassinated or not re-elected, my refugee status will become problematical. If Cardenas were to lose power, there is the potential for countless numbers of Mexicans becoming alienated from a community of shared meanings. When this happens, the inescapable human dichotomies will become unbearable and will produce disintegrative persecution. This inevitably happens because people, trying to escape these existential dichotomies, embrace one side and reject the others.

The Stalinist Mexican Communist Party represents one of these sides.

Like in all cases, I should realize that fear is a reaction to situations that may happen in the future, whether realistic or not, and is always uncomfortable. In it we find one of the contradictions of fear itself: when it should keep us from distress, it is bleakness itself.

The world goes on, outside of my tower. As the Mexican poet Octavio Paz said, "Solitude is the profoundest fact of the human condition. Man is the only being who knows he is alone, and the only one who seeks out another."

As the Mexican nationalistic sentiments would have it, solitude and sin are resolved in communion and fertility. If a society is stagnant or unavailing it must create a redemption myth, which is fertility myth and creation myth combined.

If only the Mexicans could rightly understand what charismatic use they could make of their imagination, poignancy, and originality, they would be able to gain more of an understanding of the most beautiful joys of life; a passionate desire which could make them the warm patroness of a cold world.

21

In the Soviet Union, the GPU is not only feared by the workers, but by the entire population, as the instrument that Stalin uses to maintain his bureaucracy and keep him in power. We are the masters of bribery, terror, prisons, execution, indirection, and criminality, in order to suppress and silence the population, inside and outside of our borders.

We are the most daring of the Communist Party. We are higher in authority than the Comintern and control their policies and activities. Our resources are limitless and we obey orders without the slightest hesitation.

There is a division of labor in our delictums. Agents carry out the specialized aspects of the assignments, while the press of the Communist Party, its rhetoricians, and sympathizers, serve as protective covers for our activities, diffusing any inquirendo.

By the time I arrived in Mexico, it became clear to me that the GPU was at the same time sending more of its gunmen, through the Mexican Embassy in Paris. Mexico was a large city where one could easily elude surveillance and was the perfect place to hide large numbers of GPU agents in this part of the hemisphere. There was no doubt that Stalin was building a force here.

What the GPU had failed to do was to contain the division of labor between the artists and intellectuals, and gunmen like myself.

David Alfaro Siqueiros: Journal

have always been a man of action. My involvement in political activism, since an early age, has been without equal in regard to a Mexican intellectual frame of reference. By the age of fifteen, I was leading a student strike at the San Carlos Academy of Fine Arts, to force a change in teaching methods. It lasted six months and ended in victory for the students.

Shortly after this, I conspired with a group of students and workers to overthrow the military dictator, General Victoriano Huerta. I was a contributor to La Vanguardia, the newspaper of the anti-Huerta Constitutionalist movement. I served four years as a combatant in the Revolution and attained the rank of Captain. In 1918, in Guadalajara, I organized a contingent called the Congress of Soldier Artists.

I started to travel outside of Mexico, first traveling to Spain where, in 1921, I published a magazine called Vida Americana. After returning to Mexico a year later, I was elected secretary general of Mexico's Revolutionary Painters, Sculptors and Engravers Union. Shortly after this, Diego Rivera, Javier Guerrero, and I started the union-sponsored weekly called El Machete. This would later become the official organ of Mexico's Communist Party.

Back in Guadalajara, I became heavily involved in union activities of the Miners Union and the Jalisco Workers Federation. I was thrown into jail several times for my work and in 1931 was confined to Taxco under the status of "internal exile."

It was only when Cardenas came to power that I was once again welcome in Mexico. I was also free to travel.

They say that, typically, people who are easily angered come from families that are splintered, turbulent, and not particularly skilled at emotional communication. I would say that the impetus for my mordancy came from the Marist fathers. Like so many other Marxist and atheists in Mexico, I had an early Catholic education. Like the fathers, I believe that when I am morally right, any blocking or changing of my obligations is viewed as an unbearable indignity, which should not have to be suffered.

I do not look to God for salvation, but to Cuauhtémoc, the last Aztec king. He symbolizes the glory of Mexico.

Creativity, which has been a deliberate part of my spiritual search, may be expressed not only in aesthetics but in creative action; in a way that rallies people to confront social injustice. My soul is passionately committed to creating a better world.

Just as in the world, not all factors in a work of art are equivalent. Structure, composition, and arrangement result from the subordination of certain integrants to others. It creates a flow, and the illusion of movement that is beyond the limits of psychological time. Through this flow, the artist creates a correlation between the construction and the subordination. Art represents the interaction of this struggle: the unfolding of the temporal, pure motion. Without this enslavement, or the calculated distortion of antecedents, there can be no art.

Art itself is a cognitive function that does not need emotive involvement. Emotion was not made to facilitate art, but art was made to facilitate the expression of it: the undercurrents of arousal and fury.

22

ylvia and I had taken up residence near the Trotsky compound. Sylvia had been let into the Trotsky fold and was working for him at the residence. We had separate housing, so I could come and go freely. My explanation to her was that I needed to travel for my business.

The tricky part was that I had to convince her to introduce me to her associates as her Canadian boyfriend, Frank Jacson. At first she couldn't understand why I would use another name, but after repeating to her the importance of it many times, she finally capitulated. I emphasized to her that she needed to trust me. I explained that I didn't want my business rivals to know that I was in Mexico.

I needed to posses her. It was important, more than ever, to keep Sylvia in an emotionally dependent relationship with me: aching in heart, and despairing over the thought of my leaving her. The spiritual dimension of despair was the key to governing her.

Our relationship had been built upon her needs. Once I had discovered her vulnerable areas, I needed to convince her that my stories were true, by playing on her stereotyped expectations of reality. For example: people are reluctant to challenge another person's honesty openly. Sylvia was no different. I would disarm any of her suspicions, concerning my stories; by bring them up myself, in order to disarm her by anticipating her own doubts.

My priority was now to stick close to Sylvia's friends and wait for an opening. In order to explain my limitless source of income, I told those around me that I had a boss overseas who paid juicy commissions for my business deals.

I had not met Trotsky yet, but I was insinuating myself into his world. I started entertaining the guards at expensive restaurants. To them I was Sylvia's boyfriend. At one time, when the Rosmers, friends of the Trotsky's, were visiting, I volunteered to drive them to Veracruz when they went back to Europe.

I was starting to become a little mistrustful of Eitingon. I met with him at different times to give my report. Sometimes my mother was present. It was at these meetings that I noticed a dissimilar look in her eyes. It was almost as if she was being exploited in a subtle way that she was not aware of; similar to how infants end up being fearful of people in power to varying extents. I couldn't quite put a handle on it, but it put me on alert.

The only way that I can express it is to say that I started to feel envious toward Eitingon and his relationship with my mother. Along with this came resentment. It was arising because my emotions were becoming powerful, yet I had to suppress them. They were coupled with the feeling that I could not act them out, either from weakness or because of fear; perhaps even an element of impotence.

Obviously, the mother-child relationship can be a basic source of agony or fulfillment and from this a person has no escape, even when the child becomes a man.

If what they say — that envy is all about the pursuit of the child for the mother's breast — is true, the child will not want any competitors. It will scheme to get what it thinks it needs to survive. Well, that must have been me, because I became insatiable. I could not be satisfied with their relationship anymore because of the undercurrents inside of myself, and Eitingon became the material thing to focus this upon. He was hoarding my mother and I could only see her love existing in him. Could she not see it in me anymore? Envy and competition surely had deep roots in my irrevocable past and until now was delitescent.

I was starting to lose balance and perspective toward Eitingon. At the same time I had to realize that I too was clever, and had to maintain some self control. I had to remain silent about him, especially with mother. It would have been undiscerning to tear off my mask.

The black bile of the imagination was expressing the thought that I could only see what was enviable in Eitingon, and not my own contradistinct millstone. The Russian proverbs would have us believe that we should never mention our own advantages unless in conjunction with a lack, a burden, or an accident. Instead, what they should express is the compulsion to never to mention one's own disadvantages or bad luck.

So what keeps us from being ourselves; our own nature broadening outward and furnishing evidence of our true tastes and convictions? I say it is the fear of other people's judgment. And this is what makes us feckless and conformists. It is the great leveler of mankind; and damns us to the safekeeping of the indistinguishable.

Because my envy of Eitingon would never lack any stimuli, I had to turn these feelings into an agnostic reflex: I had to outdo him through my achievements in order to gain a fundamentally new caliber of competitive reorientation. I would only be able to do this by realizing the futility of giving my thoughts to the ungenerous comparisons between myself and him. I had to assume new and different impulses; thoughts that would increase my own appraisement, were dynamic, and trained upon the future.

Generally speaking, human beings are free to separate themselves from their past and their prospects. This is the moral climate of our sound and fury; because ultimately we are responsible for what limits us. It is our obligation to develop conceivable narratives of ourselves, determine the future domain of the possible, and guide oneself toward it.

Marcus Aurelius said, "We should also observe the nature of all objects of sense — particularly such as allures us with pleasure, or affright us with pain, or are clamorously urged upon us by the voice of self-conceit — the cheapness and contemptibility of them, how sordid they are, and how quickly fading and dead." How true when considering the aphoristic sex with Sylvia. But it is consciousness itself that can really make sense out of its deeply erotic potential; a potential for connection and intercourse at the very basis for our awareness. We are ensnared, embosomed, and hypostasized in it. I knew this when I flirted with the idea of touching and being touched by my mother.

All I could think was that this fervency I had felt for her would perhaps be the only one I would feel intensely in my whole life. And from this, the fulfilled form of my character depended. My way of thinking, my instincts and way of life, would acquire a lucidity that was incorruptible.

Was all this just tragedy then?

All we know from the dead hand of Old Time is that what we do matters; that our discretions make a difference, and that existence is an epoch-making undertaking. What is significant is the attitude one takes toward his intransigent destiny; the way in which he carries his burden, the courage he demonstrates in suffering, and the sobriety he displays in calamity.

Leonid Eitingon: Journal

I had a meeting with Gnome today. His mother Caridad was present. He seemed slightly distracted and his eyes kept darting back and forth between his mother and me. Apparently resentment has insinuated itself into his personality. It is unfortunate because he will only undervalue and diminish whatever he cannot do or have, or even equal. There surely has been a relapse of certain emotions, which no doubt are poisoning his mind. The causes and consequences I am sure point to me.

He will have to be monitored for value delusions and their corresponding value judgments. Repressed resentments often return as revenge, hatred, malice, envy, and spite.

Most people avoid feeling any anguish that claims the recognition of their own vulnerability. This is why they are so afraid to acknowledge their anger, and tend to just to deny they feel anything. But, on the other hand, there are times when the anger deep in the unconscious mind, the roots deep in childhood insecurities, can break through when coming to grips with choice and action in the midst of chaos, absurdity, and suffering.

People like this have a good sense where their unconscious wants to take them.

So there are two things that I now need to do. First, is to cut the source of Gnome's anger at the source. He needs a change of attention. With the addition of more duties that will give him entirely new meaning to our plans in Mexico; hopefully he will no longer remain irritated or feel humiliated. He needs to come to believe that my motives are not hostile but friendly.

The second thing that I need to do is to go ahead with my alternative plan involving Siqueiros.

23

David Alfaro Siqueiros: Journal

The poetry of Pushkin always seems to involve two contradictory feelings; sometimes even in the same sentence. Take for example *I ROAM THE NOISY STREETS*, which taken on the surface is supposed to represent a poet persecuted by the perception of death. His preoccupation weighs heavy upon him, but he accommodates himself to the idea of death's certainty and proceeds to praise the flowering season of life.

The impingence takes place where death is out of place: in noisy streets; busy marketplaces; congregated churches. Pushkin shows us the true extraordinariness we seek in the aesthetic experience of catharsis, through the intercourse of these two currents.

This catharsis becomes evident in drawing also. There is a different interpretation of space in drawing than in painting. Painting *forces us to make the work come to life as three-dimensional, even though we perceive the activism of the lines in a two-dimensional plane. With drawing, the incarnation of the piece remains two-dimensional. It is always dualistic — using impressions of atonality, desecration, and disproportion; all of which are employed as positive effect. The forbidding countenance of death can even be effaced by the triumph and concinnity of lines.*

The cinema has become of particular interest to me since I was in Los Angeles. Filmable Art or Pictorial Cinematographic Art represents the notion that art can be foreseen as something being filmed. I have used it as montage in my mural painting and it has influenced my use of non-traditional technologies.

In other words, I am gravitating toward a greater realism.

And what could be more real than an armed raid on the Trotsky household. Leonid Eitingon, who is coordinating the efforts, has given me the green light to proceed. I have assembled a group of comrades who served in the civil war in Spain. There are three other GPU agents who will be involved in this raid. Vittoria Codovila, an Argentinean Stalinist, is one. He operated in Spain under Eitingon, and was involved in the torture and murder of many of the POUM leaders. Pedro Cheka, who is the leader of the Spanish Communist Party in exile, is another. And finally Carlos Contreras, known to many as Vittorio Vivaldi, is with us. In Spain, he was involved in the GPU's Special Task Force under the name General Carlos.

Along with Luis and Leopoldo Arenal and Antonio Pujol, we have established a network of spies in Coyoacan, renting houses in many of the sections of the village which we sometimes only use for a day or two. Julia Barradas de Serrano, the former wife of David Serrano, along with another woman, have rented a room two blocks away from the Trotsky household, and have begun seducing the police. One of them has become so enamored with Julia, that he has given her a photograph of the entire police detail as a souvenir. David Serrano is a member of the Political Bureau of the Mexican Communist Party. He is a veteran of the Spanish Civil War and is a representative of the GPU on the Party counsel.

We have rented a partially abandoned cabin in the mountains, where I have dug a grave. It now serves as a kitchen, but it will soon hold the bodies of Leon and Natalia Trotsky.

24

Leon Trotsky: Journal

*O*ur household keeps going despite the fact that I have hardly any financial resources. My only income comes from copyrights for my books, as well as published political articles in the international press media. This meager income still allows me to support my family, and pay for the services of my secretaries, guards, and household personnel. I am raising chickens and rabbits, which helps to put food on the table.

We have had several guests here lately: Jean van Heijenoort from France, Otto Schüssler from Germany, Jan Bazan from Czechoslovakia, along with the Americans — Harold Robbins, Alex Buchman, Walter Kelly, Charles Cornell, Christy Moustakis, Robert Sheldon Harte, Joseph Hanson, and Jake Cooper.

When Alfred and Marguerite Rosmer came, they brought my grandson Vsevolod Seva Volkov, son of Zinaida, my eldest daughter. Seva's mother had committed suicide in 1933 and his father was executed in a prison camp in Siberia, during the purge. I was given custody of him. We have put Seva in the bedroom next to us. We put the Rosmers in a room in the watchtower.

I find myself surrounded with an atmosphere of solidarity, partnership and a keen desire for work, not just in my political endeavors but also in the house chores. Carmen Palma takes care of the cooking. Leobardo Fernández and his sons Octavio and Carlos, help by reinforcing the guard at night. The maid Belén Estrada, along with Melquíades Benítez, keeps the house in working order. I should not forget the services of dear Fanny Yanovich, my Russian typist. She also attends to the house after transcribing to typewriter from the cylinders of the Dictaphone for three to four hours each day.

I must concede that my life here has progressed in between constraints and security measures, but I find solace in my study. It is filled with books (almost 2,200 volumes), newspapers, magazine collections, and mail. It is a trench for my political fight and a front line to socialism. I come here every morning a little after six in the morning, after feeding the rabbits and chickens. I find their feeding a satisfactory distraction. I have come up with the most scientific formula for their diet. I also have a methodology for the inspection of the animals which checks for any signs of sickness or parasites with fastidiousness.

I stay here in the study until breakfast time. After this is finished, I return to the study and remain here for the rest of the day, dictating letters and drafts of my writing into the Dictaphone.

Some say, especially my wife, that I work too hard. It is tireless work and I usually stay at it until 9:00 or 9:30 at night, with interruptions only coming at meals and when I feed the animals again at sunset. I take a nap for about an hour after lunch and have had a bed *put in the study. This has been recommended by the doctor. The day is ended when I review the day's happenings with my collaborators. This can go late into the night.*

I have started to suffer from artery hypertension, which has been provoking intense headaches. Often they interrupt my work, causing me to cease and rest. To deal with the pain I have started drinking potassium chloride. At times I suffer from insomnia and have been given sleeping pills.

Yesterday, I was at a breaking point, and uttered out loud, "How exhausted, how exhausted!" I was alone in the study. I hope no one heard me. Then I whispered, "I can't keep on..." The senseless injury and moral exhaustion of the revolutionaries who have died filling themselves and me with infamies now fills me with an ever-abiding sorrow.

Yet, on I persevere. My life now is marked with simplicity and austerity. I do not smoke or consume alcoholic beverages, and I especially dislike it when someone smokes in my presence.

When we believe that it can be safe, sometimes Natalia, myself, our friends and guards, will go on field trips to the countryside for picnics. In three cars, we will travel at least one or two hours from the city. I love the Mexican mountains. Here I collect cactus with a spade and a hoe, to be replanted back at the household.

El Pedregal and the sierra of the state of Hidalgo are my favorite spots. Some of the cactus can weigh up to 80 kilos, but the work is a great distraction for me. Of particular interest to me is the Los Viejitos variety which are elongated and covered with white threads.

Even though I am very strict in my work discipline, I hope others can appreciate my affability and affection when we converse and joke around. It is important, regardless of our ease and comfort on these trips, that the guards remain vigilant and undistracted.

Back at the house, I like to be open with my guards and am willing to talk about any subject with them. I can remember talking with the American Jake Cooper, after the Louis-Goday boxing match. I said to Jake, "Louis knocked out Goday in six rounds. I guess it won't be long before Roosevelt takes Louis into his cabinet." We had a good laugh.

25

n 1940, the Mexican Communist Party and the Confederation of Workers of Mexico began to amplify their assaults and provocations against Trotsky in the press and at political meetings.

In the March issue of Lombardo Toledano's FUTURO, all of the Stalinist slanders against Trotsky were put into one article. Under the heading, "The Significance of Trotskyism," Trotsky was accused of being the "direct organizer of foreign counter-revolutionary intervention in Mexico." The article, written by Professor Oscar Greydt Abelenda, accused him of having connections with the Nazi Gestapo, as was brought out in the Moscow trials and had never been disproved. He was also accused of placing himself in the service of the Federal Bureau of Investigation of the United States.

The article explained that Trotsky went to the FBI because he had been expelled by the Gestapo due to links he had made with Wall Street. He had to find a new boss. The article stated, "For Trotskyism this was nothing new, since 1924 it has been found in the simultaneous service of various spy agencies, such as the British intelligence service."

The article ended with a Stalinist moral: "Today it is completely evident that Trotskyism, in Latin America, is nothing more than an agency of penetration, of confusion, of provocation, and of espionage in the service of the imperialists of Wall Street."

Lombardo Toledano's job was to function in the trade unions as a mask for GPU activity. He was to be an exponent of Stalinist policy in Mexico without holding a card in the Mexican Communist Party.

Trotsky wrote in response to this, "This is how people write when ready to change the feather for the machine gun." It could not have been more prophetic.

News of the assault came to me the same way as everybody else in Mexico. I heard about it on the radio and was caught completely off guard.

Around four in the morning on May 24, 1940 a group of about twenty men attacked the police corps outside of the Trotsky household. They approached them dressed as other policemen. Siqueiros was wearing a false mustache and dark glasses. Shouting, "Viva Almazon!" they bound all five, and proceeded to cut the telephone cables. The reference to Almazon provided an opportunity to cast guilt upon the candidate opposed by the Stalinists.

The guard who was on duty that night was the American Robert Sheldon Harte. One of the disguised policemen had previously made himself acquainted to Harte. He was a trusting type of fellow. He said to Harte, "Bob, these officials have a message of extreme importance for Trotsky." Bob then opened the gate for the armed gang and they breached the patio. Their mission was to assassinate Trotsky and to burn the house.

There were two beds in Trotsky's bedroom. Over one of them, on a peg, was Natalia's straw hat. Across from the beds was a table. On the right side were pictures of Trotsky and Natalia's sons: Leon and Sergei Sedov. . In the middle was a photograph of Natalia Sedova, and left of this was one of Seva Volkov with Alexandra Moglina, along with one of Trotsky's first wife, Alexandra Sokolovskaya.

The assailants took positions at different angles in the garden. They first started opening fire on the guardhouse with machine guns, and then proceeded to the main house.

Trotsky awoke hazily, hearing what he thought were fire-crackers. It was a time on the calendar when the people of Coyoacan were celebrating special days. He became suspicious when he noticed that the explosions were too frequent and much too close. Then he smelled the acrid smell of powder. Natalia was already out of bed. They huddled in a corner of the bedroom, with Natalia shielding her husband's body with her own. He insisted that they lie flat on the floor without moving. Bullets ripped through the door, just missing them as they thudded into the wall. The cover fire held back the bodyguards in their quarters.

Bullets were now coming through the windows of the bedroom and the door, resulting in crossfire. The firing lasted three to five minutes. There were over two hundred shots fired, with nearly one hundred landing just above where the Trotskys were lying.

In the next bedroom, the grandchild Seva, alarmed by the shooting, moved his cot away from the wall, lay down on the floor, and hid in a corner of the room. A bullet grazed his right toe. One of the assailants entered the room and Seva heard him say, "Here are the bombs." Thinking that they were going to blow up the house, he rushed out of his hiding place, almost ran over the thug when flying through the door, ran toward the patio and started to shout to his grandfather that they were going to blow up the house. He then headed to the office, passed the dining room and climbed down the terrace until he reached the guard, Harold Robbins', room. Here he remained safe.

Moments later an incendiary bomb was tossed into the second bedroom and flared up next to a small cabinet. Natalia saw the figure of a man stand at the entrance to their bedroom who unleashed several rounds into each of the empty beds. This assassin had been assigned to make a final check. He mistook the pile of clothes on the bed for bodies and left.

Then there was silence.

Natalia was able to quickly extinguish the flames in Seva's room with rugs and blankets. The intruders had attempted to destroy Trotsky's archives with another incendiary device, but it failed.

They took off with the two automobiles owned by Trotsky.

The guards and secretaries ran to Trotsky's quarters to see if he was still alive, to assess the damage, and see if there were any losses. The only member that was missing was Robert Sheldon Harte, who had left with the assailants.

Ramirez Diaz, one of the bound policemen, later stated that Harte was marched through the door when they left, his arms pinned by the assailants. He was protesting, but did not seem to be struggling. His impression was that Harte was going with them voluntarily.

Whether the guards had shot any of the intruders was never ascertained, as it was a rule of the GPU to never leave behind dead or wounded who might be able to compromise the Stalinist organization.

When the police arrived at the crime scene, the officer in charge, Colonel Leandro Sánchez Salazar chief of the Mexican Secret Service, was taken aback by how calm and serene Trotsky was when narrating the events. This gave him a suspicious feeling about Trotsky, considering how inept the attack had been; there being so many bullets fired and no one hurt except Seva. His initial hypothesis, fueled by the Stalinist press, was that Trotsky had organized the event himself, to discredit his enemies. In order to throw off the investigation, the GPU set forward two alibis. First, was for the Communist Party to deny any involvement. And secondly, was to encourage the idea that Trotsky had indeed organized the attack himself.

That the attack had been prepared well in advance as was evidenced by the tools and police uniforms that were found in the abandoned Dodge, the police retrieved in one of the exclusive districts of Mexico City.

Left at the scene were scaling ladders, an electric saw, rope ladders, several incendiary devices, and a defective bomb containing enough dynamite to have blown up the entire house. This would indicate that the complicity of a guard at the entrance was not the only plan of attack.

Of course it was clear that anyone familiar with Stalin's desire to have Trotsky eliminated, would have come to the conclusion that this assault was to be the epilogue to the Moscow Show Trials. During the events of the Second World War, Stalin believed that the death of Trotsky would pass without ebullition.

26

Leonid Eitingon: Journal

$\mathcal{O}\!\!\mathcal{S}$iqueiros and his gang have launched an assault on Trotsky. They botched the job and now we have to cover their tracks. Siqueiros must have thought he was in one of his beloved American gangster movies. He went in with guns blazing. This did not turn out as I had planned. I did not expect Siqueiros to think that he was Al Capone.

I had met with Valentin Campa (a veteran member of the Mexican Communist Party), along with Raphael Carillo (a member of the Central Committee), and Herman Laborde (the Party's general secretary), to inform them of "an extremely confidential and delicate affair." I told them of the plan to kill Trotsky and asked for their help in the task of carrying out the operation.

They told me that they thought Trotsky was finished politically and rejected the proposal. I set the plan in motion anyway. I had to *leave it to Siqueiros to put his own team together with some of my GPU men, without any support.*

I think Trotsky sees himself as the popular idol of socialism and a folk hero in Latin America. I guess that even illusions cannot exist without a cause, and men are just as ready to die for an illusion as for reality.

What I need to implement now is a campaign of slander in our press media that we can control. I have also instructed the poet Pablo Neruda to obtain a Chilean visa for Siqueiros, in case he needs to make an escape from the country.

Intellectuals can have erratic and anomalous personalities, but they are our best recruits. They are especially prone to a naïve and vain, yet politically applicable, semblance of envy-avoiding behavior. It is in the shadow part of their personalities. These highly educated people are unable to claim their own identities, and opt for the philosophically wrought, long-term communist program: especially the more unequal, eminent and remarkable they are in society. The recipe is a combination of privilege with a sense of guilt. The consequence is that I end up attending to the mental set of leading artists, actors, scientists, and psychiatrists.

What I need is a network of stronger souls: those in whom a measure of resolution can easily suppress their intensity. These types of people equip their wills to fight their abandon with the proper weapons; not just having one set of passions provided to repulse another set.

For the weakest souls belong to those who constantly allow themselves to be carried away by fresh passions. The will is pulled first to one side and then to the other. When one fights a duel with oneself, the soul degenerates to its most pitiable predicament. It is unable to test its own true strength.

So far we have been able to steer the police investigation away from the facts. In conjunction with our slander campaign, two of Trotsky's secretaries (steering any attention away from Sylvia Ageloff) have been brought to jail for questioning. Two of the house-hold friends have been held for several days in the Guadalupe prison. The house of Frida Kahlo has also been searched, after we spread the rumor that Diego Rivera organized the assault jointly in connection with the Dies Committee in the United States.

Because we had failed to kill Trotsky, we now have to destroy him morally. In El Popular, we are maintaining that the attack was, "an assault on Mexico." It is a way to distance our press if the assailants are ever captured. If they never get caught, we can proceed with the "self-assault" theory.

This has become more difficult since the discovery of Robert Sheldon Harte's body. We have murdered him in the typical GPU manner, by putting a pistol bullet in the base of his brain, followed by another one in the temple. Siqueiros and his men have dumped the body in the grave that they had dug for Trotsky, up in the mountains.

In El National, we have published a story, "Trotsky Contradicts Himself," which paints him as a coward, in contradiction to Trotsky's explanation of the events. In the meantime, all of the assassins with direct links to the Kremlin have gotten out of the country.

27

Leon Trotsky: Journal

The slanderous attacks of "self-assault" by the Stalinist press have not stopped, but Stalin's agents are now also going after Bob Harte, charging that he was the leader of the gang. This is pure fiction. I cannot believe that he would have "sold out" to the Stalinists and betray me.

Bob put up a fierce resistance to the armed gang, but that has appeared in only one report. This would lead me to the conclusion that this information is being suppressed. I have been informed that he was bound and gagged by the assailants, while energetically protesting.

These are the charges being argued by the Stalinist press:

~ Bob had a photograph of Stalin in his room. It was affectionately signed by Stalin.

~ He is actually not an American, but a Russian.

~ *This Russian, who had just arrived in the country two weeks prior to the assault, had such impeccable credentials that I did not even check them out.*

~ *His luggage was covered with labels from Moscow.*

~ *He was a typical gangster type.*

~ *He had been paid a tremendous sum for his betrayal.*

~ *Bob had control of the keys to the cars used for the getaway.*

~ *He was in my confidence and led the "self-assault."*

~ *He is still alive and living at his father's house in New York.*

They cannot even keep their stories straight.

Still, the police are being steered in the wrong direction. Informants tell me that the culprit could possibly be a lawyer named Bassols, a former ambassador to France and well-known Stalinist.

This all clearly has the stamp of Stalin. By blaming the attack on me, he is doing the same thing that he did in 1933, when blaming the burning of the Reichstag by the Nazis on the Communist Party. They have even charged that the assault was organized by agents of the American Dies Committee, with the help of Almazon's Party, the purpose of which was a "provocation" as "part of the program of the oil companies."

28

*T*rotsky took the offensive, and on May 31 issued a statement that categorically implied that the police investigation had taken a wrong turn. He suggested that the GPU was involved and described our well-known methods. He also advocated that the police investigate Lombardo Toledano and David Alfaro Siqueiros, suggesting that they could "cast light on the preparation of the attempt." President Cardenas now became involved, and this brought about a turn which proved instrumental to catching the intruders.

Trotsky's article certainly made an impression and the Stalinist writers now had to go to work, calling the attack, "an international outrage." Harry Block wrote an article casting doubt on the actuality of the assault. His mimeographed paper was distributed in the United States by the Stalinist "Workers' University." He was the liaison agent between Lombardo

Toledano and GPU officer, Oumansky, who was the acting ambassador to the United States. In this article Block wrote that Trotsky was, "an instrument in the Yankee war of nerves against Mexico."

The American periodical, *The Nation*, picked up this story and published the GPU report from Mexico. *The Nation* often gave place to Stalin's desideration in critical periods and well-timed opportunities. This chance was no different.

David Serrano and Luis Mateos Martinez were arrested in concurrence with the police investigation. The Communist Party protested saying, "Our Party considers itself outside of all suspicion, since it is a revolutionary party which supports the government of General Cardenas." They added: "…since the Marxist movement does not believe in terrorism."

Caridad Meracder: Journal

Control is a perception!
Am I setting myself up for unhappiness? Because it seems to be leading to disappointment, anger, resentment, rage, and the like. Expectation has become the greatest source of embitterment. After my last assignment, I am beginning to realize that my expectations may be unrealistic.

Along with Julia Barradas de Serrano, I was set up in a house near the Trotsky household. Our job was to seduce the police squad assigned to guard the perimeter and gain intelligence about their detail. Have I become a whore?

I certainly could feel a sense of control when the different men were between my legs and extolling me with reverence. I do not deny that I enjoy the nymphomaniacal field-work of the female operative, but as I have matured, I realize that I may not have any real external control. We may be able to influence other people, but we cannot actually control them. This is the illusion of control.

Am I setting myself up for self-contradiction?

I want to shift the responsibility for my feelings to Leonid, and blame him for my unhappiness.

The strange thing is that when a man's penis becomes nothing more than a mechanical device, my will and pleasure become unlimited. When my lover is on top of me, I have trained my mind to stop reacting, and to answer in kind. It is an adaptive response to denunciation. At first I feel anger; then I remember that it is often accompanied by ideas that, when reflected on, can make me laugh.

But as Seneca said, "There is nothing useful in anger, nor does it kindle the mind to warlike deeds; for virtue, being self sufficient, never needs the help of vice."

Yet the results of hostile impulses can be imagined, sometimes with evil consequences, and followed to their end until finally one is selected that seems most fitting. One day I will find one of these policemen and put a bullet in the base of his brain.

That is a situation in which I will have complete control. A woman has ovaries and a uterus; distinctive features that can imprison her in an internal reality. But I will not allow this to parenthesize me within the capacity of my own nature.

Joseph Stalin: Journal

*N*ews of the failed attempt on my enemy is disturbing. This Trotsky is trying my patience. I want him dead.

Do we not come into the world all enemies? The Marxists with their ties of brotherhood and supposed virtues claim that this is not so. They have rendered the nature of man to be contrary to what it truly is: bestial and savage. We only have to look at the story of mankind to understand that everything is subject to change. No social conventions or rituals, political fabrications or moral fanaticisms are secure and unmodifiable.

Their impotence and invalidity resulted from the self-avowed ties of brotherhood that the Marxist invented during their tenure of grievousness.

When the Marquis de Sade spoke of the Christians, he said, "Now, I ask whether such would be the situation if they did truly exist, this supposed tie of brotherhood and the virtues it enjoins? Are they truly natural? Were they inspired in man by Nature's voice, men should be aware of them at birth. From that time onward, pity, good works, generosity, would be native virtues against which it would be impossible to defend oneself, and would render the primitive state of savage man totally contrary to what we observe it to be."

It is only ignorance to believe that socialism in Russia should never change. That which is in line with the bureaucracy should be maintained, while all that has grown old and is mildewed, should be purged.

Who but Trotsky can protest? I have eliminated well over a million voices, yet in Mexico is the one active voice I can not endure.

"THROW TROTSKY AND HIS BAND OUT OF MEXICO," was the headline of *La Voz de Mexico*. This Communist Party weekly declared that it was, "improper that a chief of police should permit a Trotsky to tell the police what they must do to discover the authors of the 'attempt.'"

As hard as we tried to cover for Siqueiros' botched job, the police announced that they had solved the case on June 18. David Alfaro Siqueiros, who at one time had been called "the Honor of Mexico," was named as the leader. Twenty-seven others were also arrested in connection with the assault, including comrade Haikys, who was part of the Soviet legation in Mexico, and former ambassador to Spain. Carlos Contreras was arrested, but the Arenal brothers and Antonio Pujol had escaped the country. Siqueiros was caught and actually boasted about his role.

The Communist Party in Mexico alternated between calling him a hero and disassociating themselves from him. They were embarrassed by the way the raid had been muffed; the assailants tripping over their own feet. They were "uncontrollable elements" and "agents provocateurs."

29

Harold Robbins: Journal

came to Mexico from the United States to defend Leon Trotsky from the brutal reality of Stalin's terrorist machine, the GPU. They are the garbage of the Revolution.

I cannot help but have a feeling of guilt and regret concerning the attack on the compound. So many things could have been done differently in our defenses. If only I had known.

Trotsky had initially resisted some of the additional security that I had proposed. I wanted a guard to be stationed by him at all times. When I look back, the lack of adequate security checks was to have calamitous consequences. Our resources were limited and Trotsky believed that too much suspicion and worry about infiltration, would be counter-productive. Before the attack, he was disinclined to subjecting people to searching enquiries and investigation. Even Natalia said, "It is impossible to convert one's life solely into self-defense, for in that case life loses all its value."

This sense of aversion made many of us feel ill at ease. It created doubt and unwillingness to increase security. But now we are hopefully habituated by a previous sense of loss.

Before the attack I was starting to feel some discontent with my role here. As a volunteer I had traveled a long distance and suddenly found myself doing something totally different from what I had imagined.

I expected some degree of accountability and fulfillment from my work. I found myself with too much free time and with a mission that was not quite clear. I just hope that this did not cause me to be sloppy in my work. If so, this will not happen again. Our security is of top priority now.

Leon has said to me that the work he is now engaged in is the most important work of his life. According to him, it is even more important than 1917 or the Civil War.

I have to say that I was caught completely off guard during the attack. Not because it happened, but by how I reacted when it occurred. It happened so fast that it didn't actually register in my consciousness until it almost ended. I found myself in an unexplained state of excitement before I even realized what was happening. And now, I find myself fearing and reacting to people and events that are completely harmless in a much more aggressive way. I am associating various things through this recent experience, and I consider it beneficial. I am on my toes.

I feel a distraction of the will by the compulsion of fury in one direction; and also feel like being pulled in multifarious directions by passion and ideals. I have found, though, that it is through weakness and loss that I have discovered the true nature of identity and authenticity.

Nevertheless, in view of Trotsky's vital and all-important work, there will inevitably be another attempt on his life. Yet, there are serious deficiencies in the security, and more stalwart initiatives should be implemented. I have taken it upon myself to make sure that the house's defenses be strengthened and new precautions taken.

Natalia Sedova: Journal

atred always accompanies envy. It is rarely felt so impetu-ously as when in relation to somebody else's inborn abilities and gifts. What Stalin envies most of Lev is his specific genius. No other disgrace can so thoroughly abase, diminish, and invalidate a person. Not the least of its symptoms is the qualitative pettiness and meanness.

Emmanuel Kant wrote that envy is a natural impulse, "inherent in the nature of man, and its only manifestation makes of it an abominable vice, a passion not only distressing and tormenting to the subject, but intent on the destruction of the happiness of others, and one that is opposed to man's duty towards himself as towards other people."

In Richard III, Gloucester has seen into the intense nihility; that chasm at the still point of mere existence, where all is accorded and nothing is sincere. Stalin has this appetite: of the universal wolf. He wants to demolish the pilgrim's staff and philosophies we depend on to keep from finding ourselves at that abyss.

The only aspect of envy that is not contumelious is that of faith in a great cause. Here; this is the envy one feels for people who have a true and deep and intellectual lifework that brings them through the most sinister pitfalls — including death. I quietly harbor this form.

Lev has often inveighed against my foreboding, since the attack. "You see, they didn't kill us last night, and yet you are still dissatisfied," he would say to me in the morning, after opening the sturdy steel shudders recently built in the bedroom. Sometimes he would add, "Well, now no Siqueiros can get at us."

Our house has become a fortress. The Socialist Workers Party has contributed six thousand dollars to this project. The surrounding wall has been raised, surveillance towers built, and the windows above Morelos Street have been partially blocked off. Most of the windows and doors have been replaced by narrow armored doors that can be secured with heavy metal locks. The alarm system has been updated and now only the study and the office have open doors to the yard.

Lev says that it looks like a medieval prison.

Always eager for a good day's work, Lev still attends to the rabbits in the morning. This is something that he will not give up, even when feeling poorly. He says that he commiserates with the little animals. It clears his mind from distractions, but it fatigues him physically. He feeds them, along with the chickens, from a quarter past seven till nine o'clock. When he has an idea he will take time to interrupt his work to dictate his thoughts into the Dictaphone. He needs to reserve his energy for the truly necessary work; at his desk. He becomes completely absorbed in whatever he does, be it on the patio or at his desk. But we must be careful. He has to be on guard at all times.

It is a shame that we cannot go on our war-expeditions for cacti, the way we used to. It is because of "circumstances beyond our control," as L.D. puts it.

It fills me with happiness when I see L.D. in good spirits. I saw him at his desk, after a siesta, and it was covered with research for a case he was working on. He was working on a rebuttal to another slanderous charge, but he was energetic, despite his occasional bouts of enervation. When I peeked through the door, I could see him bent over — looking like Pimen, the monk-scribe in Pushkin's Boris Godounov.

30

fter the Siqueiros assault, I had a meeting with Eitingon: "Ramón, the time has come," he said.

"Why wasn't I informed of the assault?" I asked.

"It was deemed prudent to keep you out of it for certain reasons. You surely know that we often have several contingent plans in effect for our operations. What we needed was for you to remain close to Ageloff and when we needed you to act, we would then set in motion your attempt. That time is now."

"I see," I responded. "There could be a problem, though."

"And what would that be?"

"You have to understand, that they have increased security so much after Siqueiros' attack, that it is practically impossible to gain entrance to the household now."

"Okay Ramón, but understand this — you need to get in somehow, no matter how. Stalin is getting impatient and all of our jobs are on the line. That means our lives are on the line."

"Leonid, I'm just not sure. I just don't think I can do it."

He looked at me in a strange and menacing way. Taking a folder from his briefcase, he slid it across the table toward me.

"Take a look inside," he directed.

I opened the folder and saw a picture inside. It was a picture of a woman who was naked and tied up with rope. Her head was lowered, so I could not see who it was.

"Next!" Leonid said, indicating that I should continue to the next photograph.

In the next picture, the woman's head was raised. She had a look of fear in her eyes and a tear streaming down her cheek. It was my mother. My breathing stopped. For the briefest of moments, I was in a state of shock.

"What is this?" I asked.

"This is what we have come to Ramón. We have your mother and we are going to kill her if you don't follow through with the assassination of Trotsky. Time is running out. I want you to know something Ramón; Caridad's death is going to be painful. But first, she is going to be raped brutally. Can you picture this Ramón? It is not going to be pretty."

My heart started to race; my breathing was fast; and my muscles were tensing. My first response was to jump across the table and choke Eitingon to death, but I couldn't move. I was paralyzed. The room suddenly seemed as cold as Siberia. I wanted to say something, anything, but my mouth became dry and I was having trouble swallowing. A numbing and tingling sensation spread over me.

I scanned the restaurant for signals of danger, and then I spotted two men by the entrance. There was another by the back exit.

Conscious mental activity is slow, because it operates independently of consciousness. This is why our rational decisions usually take place after our quicker emotional reactions. I was about to put myself in danger of making bad decisions, especially when you consider that all emotions are impulses for action.

I could only, at first, take a defensive posture, which in retrospect was a fear-motivated response of angry aggression. Then I switched to planning how I could harm Eitingon, or at least cause some degree of fear in him. There was definitely an imbalance of power, though. He held all the cards. There was an arms-race between my neural responses.

When we react, we gauge people and situations as vile, sick, grotesque, or malevolent. Then when we characterize the outcome of the situations we find ourselves in as unimaginable, senseless, unfair, or unjust. We are at the mercy of this unpredictable and powerful emotion: anger.

"If you touch a hair on her head, I will kill you," was what popped out.

"You need to redirect your anger, and make sure that you know for what purpose it is serving you now. You need to use it to get the job done. You are a resourceful man, Ramón. Use it to get into the house. It will take only one brief moment to deliver a lethal strike against Trotsky to kill him. It will have to be up close and personal," he said coldly, while looking directly in my eyes.

I had been so wrong to believe that I was entitled to a sense of fairness from him. I had the mistaken idea that my mother and I were special to him. It was at this moment that I realized the universe is indifferent and that maintaining that things be fair was purely irrational.

"Verschiebung," he said.

"What?"

"It is a German word. It refers to when the emotive tendencies are inhibited. I was fully aware of how you would react,

Ramón, so I had no other choice but to make sure you would not behave in some more drastic fashion, if the restraints were off. I have no other choice but to make it clear to you that if you do something stupid, Caridad dies. I will not hesitate and will put the bullet in her brain myself."

I tried to think of a cutting remark, but could not.

I was entombed in the sphere of the between; where people merge, truly merge, without the hypocrisy of subterfuge and speciousness.

*T*he guards already knew me, because I had entertained them at expensive restaurants, several times since Sylvia and I came to Mexico. I had remained aloof about Trotsky with her, in order to keep my cover safe. But now I had to put everything into motion, and I had to do it quickly. I started to show sympathy toward Trotskyism and I told her that I wanted to meet him, under the pretext of having him look at an article I had written, concerning the polemics among the comrades from the Socialist Workers Party. If he read the text, he could make some observations in order to make it better.

The first meeting was to be a dress rehearsal for the actual assassination.

I met Trotsky in his office shortly after Sylvia made the request. I made mental notes about the office. Light came in from the garden, coming down from the balcony, through a stained glass window. He sat at his desk. It was covered with books and pamphlets, along with some typed sheets of paper, a pencil case, two inkwells, a desk dry pad, scissors, a small briefcase, and cylinders of wax for the Edison Dictating Machine, which was next to the desk. On the left side of the desk was a shelf containing dictionaries and reference books. There were two other large bookshelves in the room that were full of books. I noticed the names Lenin and Marx, and Engels written in Russian, on several spines. There were at least eighty or more volumes of the Russian encyclopedia — *Brockhaus and Efron*. In the corner was a bed.

I sat on the edge of the desk, always keeping myself above his level. I had to see if he objected to this, for it was from above that I would strike the fatal blow.

I was offended when he said that he considered my article to be "banal to an embarrassing degree and devoid of interest." I had to keep control of the situation, and assured him that I would take his advice and improve what I had written. It was clear that he was only doing it for Sylvia.

Throughout our lives, we invent different ways of gaining reinforcement from others. Most of mine came from my early life experiences and reflected times when I would feel powerless. This I knew well; so dealing with the situation came easier to me than I had thought it would. The combination of the emotional and behavioral bearing, and the predictable responses between Trotsky and me was simple for me to impose upon. By the time I walked out of the office, Trotsky had given me his time and advice. I was scheduled to come back with my revisions. Soon he would be dead.

It's funny, I actually remember what he told me about my article. I didn't really put much effort into it, but he was attentive and exacting. He told me that the denial of an effective outlet for exhibiting political opposition has led to more extreme resistance movements that are organized and unfulfilled. Even though there may be no immediate solution present, it was clear that the groundwork of discontent must be appealed to and that just suppressing the opposition was not the solution.

Natalia Trotsky: Journal

The Canadian with the French accent, Harold Jacson, called on us today. Lev told me that he was wearing a topcoat and a hat. I guess he felt the need to tell me this, because he sensed some new feature about the man. Lev told me that Jacson surprised him by his conduct. He mentioned it in such a way that would indicate that he did not want to elaborate on it, but still felt that he should mention it to me.

He said that Jacson had brought an article of his to be looked at. In reality, he termed it as just a few muddled phrases.

I am worried after Lev related to me that, "He did not resemble a Frenchman at all. He suddenly sat down on my desk, all the while keeping his hat on."

"Truly strange, I have never seen him wearing a hat," I answered.

"This time he wore a hat," Lev responded, pursuing the subject no further, and seeming in no hurry to draw any conclusions.

31

Leon Trotsky: Journal

The twentieth century will never discover where fulfillment
or satisfaction lies until it gives up its attempt to demonstrate that men and women are not human. The
discontent of human beings is not to be rationalized on the same
proposition as the wretchedness of the starving dog or dehydrated posy.
Certainly human life can suffer affliction and tribulation, but it is
focused on principles from which our essence ascends: through the
intellect, the will, and the soul.

Within us there is a pull between the autonomous and
conformity. This creates a conflict. We want to become our self-deter-
mined selves, yet want to be included in the larger organic unity. Our
culture determines the extent of our wholeness. But our self-aware-
ness, which helps us define what makes us original and revolutionary,

makes us feel guilty and anxious about our singleness, detachment, and ultimately our frailty.

The intellect alone is not enough to achieve happiness. We must include the will; to be brought into co-partnership. There can be neither happiness without bravery nor moral fiber without striving. Strength is the presupposition of all morality; authenticated by those who are frail by nature and dynamic by will.

What separates man from beast is passion. It is both gift and burden. It implies suffering, endurance, and submission. This happens, because we are forced to surrender to passions: we do not choose them; they possess us — reveling in their roily intensity and afflictive intelligence. They endure, surviving all impediments.

My job now is to settle unfinished business. To do this, I must mine the quarry of the heart's core. The obstinacy to forgive, the iron will to love, and the conviction to inquire after what diminishes me, will help me to do this; to tie the loose ends of associations, unions, and alliances; from person to person, friend to friend, and from idea to idea.

If only men could develop a hunger for one of the unequaled delights in life — an intoxicated curiosity which would dispose them to forget everything else; and they could make awe-inspiring use of their creative imaginations, illumination, originality, and "thick coming-fancies."

I am Russian. In Russia we draw from wisdom, patience, isolation and stolidity. We use these peculiarities to master our internality, so that we can transcend our anguish. The transformation from suffering and endurance comes through sagacity and cultivation.

In Mexico, they draw from salutary sentiments with emotional coloring, communal initiative, and positive lives; which seems to maximize pleasure and minimize suffering. Suffering is considered an

alien and intrusive insinuation on their happy lives. They prevail over
suffering through positive mental attitude.

I am the only one left to arm the revolutionary international
working class with the ideas of the Opposition, while the skeptics and
cowardly abandon Marxist stands and make their peace with Stalinism
or capitalism.

I am a citizen of the planet now, yet it is a planet with no visa.

On the afternoon of the twentieth of August, two days after my first meeting, I was to see Trotsky alone for a short consultation, despite the apprehensiveness of the guards and his wife. It was a stroke of luck for me to be able to have an audience with Trotsky, because he was by this time surrounded by guards at all times.

The household was expecting a new visitation and were prepared for it with the additional security measures. They were convinced that Stalin, having suffered moral and political humiliation after the failed attempt, would now have to show that he was powerful enough to carry out his will. Fortunately, they did not make more efforts to check up more thoroughly on me, especially since I believe that several members of the household had reservations about me.

Sylvia told me that Trotsky had not lost his sense of humor, with all of the security he lived in. He would say things to his wife like, "We have survived a whole night without being murdered...and you are still not happy." She complained that there wasn't enough security. Then he would go on and say, "We have been given another day of life, Natasha." It was his affectionate name for her.

I had taken a mountain climbing axe and sawed off most of the handle. I would conceal it under my coat. After my dry run, I was sure that I would not be questioned about wearing a coat, since they were now used to seeing me in one.

I arrived at the house and was let in through the front entrance. I was escorted through the entrance hallway, which led to the garden and the henhouses in the back. Through the garden, I walked past the climbing roses, cacti, and several patches of daisies. Trotsky was standing in front of an open rabbit hutch. He was feeding the animals. We greeted each other.

I was wearing my hat and had the coat over my arm, hiding the axe. I held it close and tight to my body. I was extremely nervous and had a hard time keeping myself from shaking. Natalia approached us from the patio. Removing my hat, I turned towards her. "I'm very thirsty; may I have a glass of water?" I asked after our greetings. My throat had become so dry I could barely speak. I just had to focus and keep collected.

"Would you prefer some hot tea?" she asked.

"No thank you. I just ate a short while ago and feel that the food is stuck here," I said pointing to my throat.

She started to ask me why I was wearing a hat and coat on a day when it was not raining. Panic rushed through my body. "Yes, this is true, but it won't last long. It might rain," was all I could come back with.

It seemed as if she wanted to pursue the point, but finally let it drop. I was really worried because of boasting in the past about never wearing a hat and coat. I was working against time, and had to improvise. If I didn't, my mother was going to be executed. The problem with lying is keeping all of your stories straight.

Natalia changed the subject and asked how Sylvia was feeling. This caught me off guard, because Sylvia was not ill. I had to stop and think for a moment. I must have seemed as if in a dream, but after coming out of it I answered, "Sylvia? Oh she is always well."

Backing away toward Trotsky, who was near the rabbit hutches, Natalia asked me if my article was ready.

"Yes, it is."

"Is it typed?" she asked. "Lev Davidovich does not like reading handwritten manuscripts."

The sun was shining brightly and I was beginning to break out in a sweat. The flowers were blooming and the grass was brilliant.

A conversation ensued about how Sylvia and I had plans to leave the next day. The Trotskys suggested that Sylvia come join us, but I made excuses. Natalia explained to him that she had already asked me for tea, but refused saying that I was not feeling too well. They asked for us to stop by the next day. I declined, saying that it was inconvenient.

Trotsky said, "Your health is poor? You don't look too well." And then he finally provided the words that I was waiting to hear. "Well, what do you say, shall we go look at the article?"

He closed the door to the hutches and methodically cleaned himself. He paid particular attention to the cleaning of his fingers. After brushing off his shirt he started to walk towards the office. I followed and Natalia did as well. It made me nervous, fearing that she would accompany us into the office. She stopped at the door, while Trotsky and I entered through the door, the article in one hand and my coat in the other. The axe was hidden underneath. I held it as tightly as I could, because it seemed that I was shaking and might have dropped it, risking discovery.

The door closed.

Natalia Trotsky: Journal

ho would have suspected it? The day was so peaceful and beautiful. How many times had I seen L.D. walk in and out of that office door, from the patio? He stepped into the office with the Canadian fiancé of Sylvia's. I was in the next room. It was only after a few short minutes, when I heard a terrible, frightening scream from Lev's office. Without thinking, I ran as fast as I could toward the commotion. The guards were already in the room and were wrestling with Jacson and beating him mercilessly. Lev was standing against the door post, blood covering his face, eyes, and glasses. His arms were dangling limply by his sides.

"Jacson," he said. "It has happened."

His legs gave way and he slouched to the floor. He was completely calm and collected in his time of crisis. He told me that Seva must be taken away. He told me that he loved me.

After I placed a pillow under his head, he said. "Don't let them kill him," referring to the guards who were beating Jacson. "We need him alive. He must confess."

He told me that Jacson wanted to strike him one more time, but Lev had turned around and fought with the assailant. I saw that one of the guards had a pistol in his hand. He started towards the office. We thought they were going to kill Jacson. Again Lev implored us not to kill him.

Jacson was crying, whimpering and complaining, "They made me do it. They have my mother."

When Trotsky turned himself towards the desk, to read my article, I removed the axe from beneath my coat. I struck him on the head as hard as I could. I expected for him to fall silently to the floor, dead. Instead he stood up and turned to me and fought. He was strong for an old man. The guards were on me before I could strike another blow.

I was excited and wailed when they started beating me. I could only think of my mother. I explained that they made me do it. After that, I never revealed who I was or who I worked for. I maintained that I killed Trotsky for personal reasons, being disillusioned with Trotskyism. I stuck with this story for twenty years.

Sylvia Ageloff: Journal

When the news that Jacques had murdered Trotsky came to me, I went into a state of shock. I couldn't believe it. This was my first response. I went numb and went around as if a robot, going through the motions of my daily life — but feeling nothing. I could not eat and was in a mode of confusion. I developed an infection in my lungs.

As time passed, other emotions plagued me: pity, regret, sorrow, shame, remorse, and fear — each emotion fully aware of and following the previous one.

How and why did I let this happen to me; to be used like this?

Before I met Jacques, I had overlooked and neglected all of the good circumstances in my life, and as a result had lost all awareness of my significance and reference. As I fell in love with him, I started to learn in each moment, how to appreciate and enjoy what being alive offered. At the same time, I simultaneously became aware of the value in myself. My self-generating negative feelings were overcome as I came to know and understand my inner personality. Oh Jacques! How could you?

Making a choice to love is the most profound resolution a person can make. Two hearts join; giving and sustaining life. Love ultimately becomes our potential and our liberation.

32.

I was in Lecumberri prison twenty years, for this crime. They took good care of me and I ate pretty well. Siqueiros had been given a light sentence. I thought that I would also, but it was not the case.

It was not until 1953 that my true identity was revealed, in spite of my silence. Through fingerprints and a chain of evidence, along with the testimony of Russian spies who defected to Western countries, I was linked to Stalin's secret terror machine.

My mother and Eitingon went back to the Soviet Union. They were awarded a bureaucratic award by Stalin, but Eitingon was eventually imprisoned after Stalin was gone. I do not know what happened to my mother after this. Some things in Russia remain secrets. I will be awarded myself when I reach home. The NKVD has now become what is called the KGB. They think I am some kind of a hero. I am not. I am just a scared man, who did what he had to do to save his mother.

I have no regrets though. I have been asked this question. To do so, would mean that I suffer from grief. No emotion is more common to our life's experiences and nothing is more natural than grief. But it does not apply to me. It weakens a person and partitions his mind. It disarranges his sleep and contaminates his dreams. It sublimates intuitive understanding. It creates a fear that you will be overcome by sorrow, and an inescapable loneliness.

Natalia Trotsky: Journal

Leon Trotsky was the most important strategist of the socialist movement. History will remember this. In his struggle against the Stalinist bureaucratic dictatorship, he became the most slandered and persecuted revolutionary on the planet. But he was not a tragic figure. The Trotsky I knew was an unwavering idealist.

If he had not been present in Petersburg during the October Revolution, the leadership of the Bolsheviks would have prevented it from happening. Lev believes that it was Lenin who was the one. I prefer to believe that it was my Lev Davidovich.

� � �

Mark Van Aken Williams received a Master of Education and a Bachelor of Arts from Cleveland State University.

He has enjoyed traveling throughout the world: including salmon fishing in Alaska, visiting Mayan ruins in the Yucatan Peninsula, deep sea fishing in Costa Rica and attending an International Rainforest Workshop on the Amazon River in Peru.

When not traveling or writing, Williams enjoys cooking for friends and family and following soccer (especially British), as well as baseball and football. His favorite sport is deep sea fishing.

The author's book of poetry, Circus by Moonlight: Poems 1990–2007, was published in 2009. Williams is currently working on another novel.

Learn more at www.markvawilliams.com.

Circus
by
Moonlight

Mark Van Aken Williams

"A perfect browse for poetry
enthusiasts... an impressive
talent and skilled wordsmith,
deserving of as wide and
appreciative an audience as possible."
—Small Press Bookwatch, The Midwest Book Review

Circus by Moonlight
Poems 1997–2007

MARK VAN AKEN WILLIAMS

"A perfect browse for poetry enthusiasts …
establishes Williams as an impressive talent
and skilled wordsmith, deserving of as wide
and appreciative an audience as possible."
~The Midwest Book Review, Small Press Bookwatch

The author's poetry reflects a sensibility that extends
beyond national borders and encompasses the
dichotomy of poverty/wealth, striving/acceptance,
ancient/modern, and the particular and universal.

ISBN-13: 978-0-9760576-6-6
ISBN-10: 0-9760576-6-2
LCCN: 2009903875

Lucky Press, LLC is a traditional, independent publishing company located in the beautiful Appalachian foothills of Athens, Ohio. Founded in 1999, it became an LLC and published its first title in 2000. From its original aim to publish books about "characters, real or imagined, who overcome adversity or experience adventure," Lucky Press has given exposure to worthwhile authors, and expanded into the categories of young adult, womens, and literary fiction and pets.

LaVergne, TN USA
12 May 2010
182496LV00003B/10/P